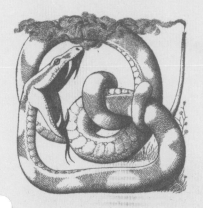

PINOCCHIO

First published in 2002 by

Simply Read Books
501-5525 West Boulevard Vancouver
BC Canada V6M 3Y3

Text copyright © 2002 Simply Read Books
Illustrations copyright © 2002 Iassen Ghiuselev

10 9 8 7 6 5 4 3 2 1

Canadian Cataloguing in Publication Data

Collodi, Carlo, 1826-1890.
The Adventures of Pinocchio

Translation of : Le avventure di Pinocchio.

ISBN 0-9688768-0-3

I. Ghiuselev, Iassen, 1964- II. Title
PZ8.C64Ad2002   j853'.8   C2001-910797-8

The Story of a Puppet

THE ADVENTURES
OF PINOCCHIO

by Carlo Collodi

Illustrated by Iassen Ghiuselev

Simply Read Books

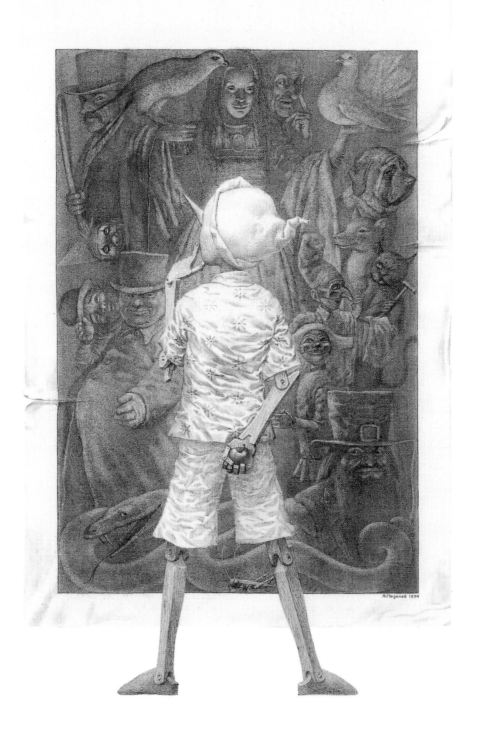

CONTENTS

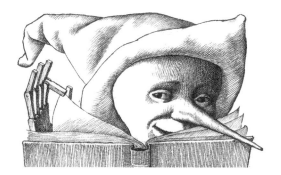

CHAPTER I

*What happened when Maestro Cherry, carpenter, found a piece of
wood that wept and laughed like a child*

Once upon a time, there was . . . "A king!" my young readers will say immediately. No, children, you are mistaken. Once upon a time, there was a piece of wood. It was not an expensive piece of wood, not at all. Just an average block of firewood, one of those thick, solid logs that are put on the fire in winter to make cold rooms cozy and warm.

I do not know how this really happened. However, one fine day this piece of wood appeared in the shop of an old carpenter. His real name was Maestro Antonio, but everyone called him Maestro Cherry, because the tip of his nose was so round and red and shiny that it looked like a ripe cherry.

As soon as he saw the piece of wood, Maestro Cherry was filled with joy. Rubbing his hands together happily, he mumbled to himself, "This has come at the right time. I will use it to make the leg of a table." He grasped the hatchet quickly to peel off the bark and shape the wood. But as he was about to give it the first blow, he stood still, with his arm lifted high, for he had heard a tiny, little voice say in a pleading tone, "Please be careful! Do not hit me so hard!"

What a look of surprise shone on Maestro Cherry's face! His funny face became still funnier. He looked around the room in fright to find out where the tiny, little voice had come from and saw no one! He looked under the bench . . . no one! He peeped inside the closet . . . no one! He searched among the shavings . . . no one! He opened the door to look up and down the street . . . and still no one!

"Oh, I see!" he then said, laughing and scratching his wig. "I guess that I only thought I heard the tiny voice say the words! Well, well . . . to work once more." He struck the piece of wood with a serious blow. "Oh, oh! You hurt me!" cried the same faraway little voice. This threw Maestro Cherry into consternation, and he just stood wide-eyed with his mouth open.

When he recovered a little, he said, trembling and stuttering from fright, "Where did that voice come from, when there is no one around? Might it be that this piece of wood has learned to weep and cry like a child? I can hardly believe it. Here it is . . . a piece of ordinary firewood, good only to burn in the stove, the same as any other. Yet, . . . might someone be hidden in it? If so, all the worse for him. I'll fix him!"

With these words, he grabbed the log with both hands and started to knock it about unmercifully. He threw it to the floor, against the walls of the room, and even at the ceiling. He listened for the tiny voice to moan and cry. He waited two minutes . . . nothing . . . five minutes . . . nothing . . . ten minutes . . . still nothing.

"Oh, I see," he said, trying bravely to laugh, and ruffling his wig. "It is easy to see how I only imagined I heard the tiny voice! Well, well—back to work again!" Poor Maestro Cherry was scared half to death, so he tried to sing a happy song in order to gain courage. He set aside the hatchet and picked up the plane to make the wood smooth and even, but as he drew it back and forth, he heard the same tiny voice. This time it giggled as it spoke, "Stop it! Oh, stop it! Ha, ha, ha! You are tickling my stomach!"

This time poor Maestro Cherry collapsed as if he had been shot. When he opened his eyes, he was sitting on the floor. His face had completely lost its composure and fright had even turned the tip of his nose from red to deepest purple.

CHAPTER II

Maestro Cherry gives the piece of wood to his friend Geppetto, who uses
it to make himself a puppet that will dance, fence, and turn somersaults

At that very instant, a loud knocking banged on the door. "Come in," said the carpenter, not having an ounce of strength left to stand up. As the words were spoken, the door opened and in stepped a lively little old man. His name was Geppetto, but to the boys of the neighborhood he was Polendina, because the wig he always wore matched the same color as polenta.

Geppetto had a very bad temper. Fear to those who called him Polendina! He became as wild as a beast and no one could control him.

"Good day, Maestro Antonio," said Geppetto. "What are you doing on the floor?"

"I am teaching the ants the alphabet."

"Good luck to you!"

"What brought you here, friend Geppetto?"

"My legs. And it may flatter you to know, Maestro Antonio, that I have come to beg you for a favor."

"Here I am, at your service," answered the carpenter, raising himself on to his knees.

"This morning a great idea came to me."

"Tell me about it!"

"I thought of making myself a beautiful wooden puppet. A wonderful puppet! One that will be able to dance, to fence, and turn somersaults. I intend to take it with me around the world, to earn my crust of bread and glass of wine. What do you think of it?"

"Bravo, Polendina!" cried the same tiny voice which came from no one knew where.

On hearing himself called Polendina, Maestro Geppetto turned the color of a red pepper and, facing the carpenter, said to him angrily, "Why do you insult me?"

"Who is insulting you?"

"You called me Polendina."

"I did not."

"I suppose you think *I* did! Yet I know it was you!"

"No!"

"Yes!"

"No!"

"Yes!"

They grew angrier each moment, went from words to blows, and finally began to scratch and bite and slap each other. When the fight was over, Maestro Antonio had Geppetto's yellow wig in his hands and Geppetto had the carpenter's curly wig in his mouth.

"Give me back my wig!" shouted Maestro Antonio in a surly voice.

"You return mine and we'll be friends."

The two little old men, each with his own wig back on his own head, shook hands and swore to be good friends for the rest of their lives.

"Well then, Maestro Geppetto," said the carpenter, to show he had no bad feelings, "what is it you want?"

"I want a piece of wood to make a puppet. Will you give one to me?"

"Gladly," answered Maestro Antonio, who immediately went to his bench to get the piece of wood that had frightened him so much. But as he was about to give it to his friend, it slipped out of his hands with a violent jerk and hit against poor Geppetto's thin legs.

"Ah! Is this the polite way, Maestro Antonio, to present your friend with a gift? You have almost crippled me!"

"I swear to you I did not do it!"

"Do you mean that *I* did it!"

"It's the fault of this piece of wood."

"You're right, but remember you were the one to throw it at me."

"I did not throw it!"

"Liar!"

"Geppetto, do not insult me or I will call you Polendina."

"Idiot!"

"Polendina!"

"Donkey!"

"Polendina!"

"Ugly monkey!"

"Polendina!"

On hearing himself called Polendina for the third time, Geppetto lost his head with rage and threw himself upon the carpenter. Then and there, they gave each other a sound thrashing. After this fight, Maestro Antonio had two more scratches on his nose, and Geppetto had two buttons missing from his coat.

Having settled their argument, they shook hands and swore to be good friends for the rest of their lives. Then Geppetto took the fine piece of wood, thanked Maestro Antonio, and limped away toward home.

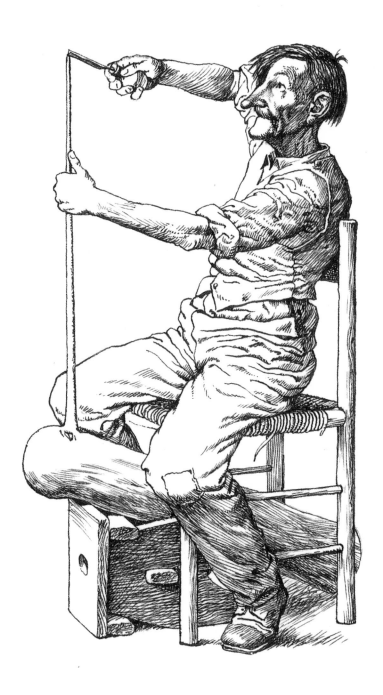

CHAPTER III

*Geppetto goes home and begins immediately to make the puppet and
names him Pinocchio. The first pranks of the puppet.*

Little as Geppetto's house was, it was neat and
comfortable. It was a small room on the ground
floor, with a tiny window under the stairway. The
furniture could not have been much simpler.
There was only a very old chair, a rickety old bed,
and a broken down table. On the wall, there was a
painting of a fireplace full of logs burning, with a
pot boiling away happily and sending up clouds of
what looked like real steam.

As soon as he reached home, Geppetto took his
tools and began to cut and shape the wood into a
puppet. "What will I call him?" he wondered. "I think I'll call him Pinocchio. This
name will bring him success. I knew a whole family of Pinocchios once. Pinocchio was
the father, Pinocchia was the mother, and Pinocchios were the children. They were all
lucky, and the richest of them begged for his living."

After choosing a name for his puppet, Geppetto started to work to make the hair, the
forehead, and the eyes. Imagine his surprise when he noticed that its eyes moved and
then stared fixedly at him. Geppetto, seeing this, felt insulted and said despondently,
"Wooden eyes, why do you stare at me?" There was no answer.

After the eyes, Geppetto made the nose, which began to stretch as soon as it was
finished. It stretched and stretched and stretched until it became so long that it seemed
endless. Poor Geppetto kept cutting it and cutting it, but the more he cut the imperti-
nent nose, the longer it grew. In despair, he let it alone. Next, he made the mouth. No
sooner was it finished than it began to laugh and poke fun at him.

"Stop laughing!" said Geppetto angrily, but he might as well have spoken to the wall.
"Stop laughing, I say!" he roared in a thunderous voice. The mouth stopped laughing,
but it stuck out a long tongue. Not wishing to start an argument, Geppetto made
believe he saw nothing and went on with his work.

After the mouth, he made the chin, the neck, the shoulders, the stomach, the arms,
and the hands. As he was about to put the last touches on the fingertips, Geppetto felt
his wig being pulled off. He glanced up and what did he see? His yellow wig was in the

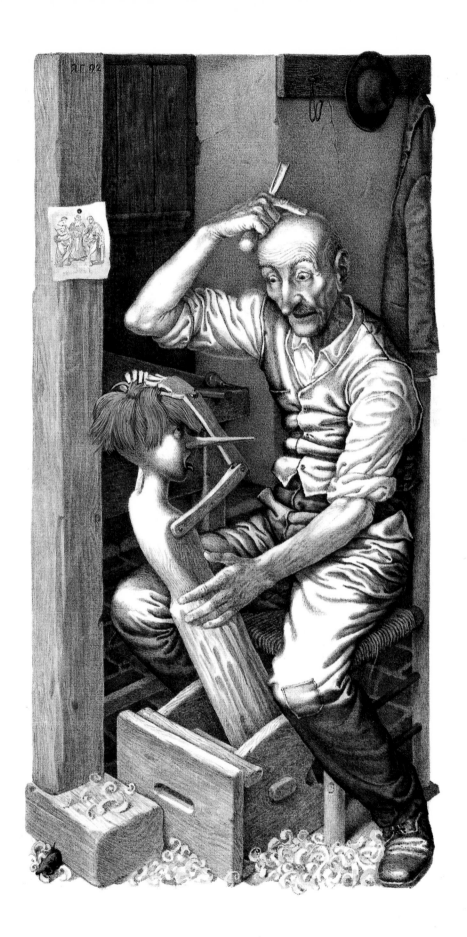

puppet's hand. "Pinocchio, give me my wig!" Instead of giving it back, Pinocchio put it on top of his own head and almost smothered himself underneath it.

This unexpected trick made Geppetto feel very sad and downcast, more so than he had ever been before. "Pinocchio, you wicked boy!" he cried out. "You are not yet finished, and you start out by being impudent to your poor old father. Very bad, my son, very bad!" he said, and wiped away a tear.

The legs and feet still had to be made. As soon as they were done, Geppetto felt a sharp kick on the tip of his nose. "I deserve it!" he thought. "I should have thought of this before I made him. Now it's too late!" He took hold of the puppet under the arms and put him on the floor to teach him to walk.

Pinocchio's legs were so stiff that he could not move. Geppetto held his hand and showed him how to put out one foot after the other. When his legs were limbered up, Pinocchio started to walk by himself and ran around the room. He came to the open door, and with one leap he was out into the street. Away he ran!

Poor Geppetto ran after him but could not catch him, because Pinocchio ran in leaps and bounds. His two wooden feet, as they beat on the stones of the street, made as much noise as twenty peasants did in wooden shoes. "Catch him! Catch him!" Geppetto kept shouting, but the people in the street, seeing a wooden puppet running like the wind, stood still to stare and laugh until they cried.

At last, by sheer luck, a carabiniere, who happened along, hearing all the noise, thinking it might be a runaway colt, stood bravely in the middle of the street with his legs firmly set apart, resolved to stop it and prevent any trouble.

Pinocchio saw the carabiniere from a distance and tried his best to escape between the legs of the big man, but without success. The carabiniere grabbed him by the nose (since it was extremely long and seemed made on purpose for that very thing) and returned him to Maestro Geppetto.

The little old man wanted to pull Pinocchio's ears. Think how he felt when, upon searching for them, he discovered that he had forgotten to make them! All he could do was to seize Pinocchio by the back of the neck and take him home. As he was doing so, he shook him two or three times and said to him angrily, "We're going home now. When we get home, then we'll settle this matter!"

Pinocchio, on hearing this, threw himself on the ground and refused to take another step. One person after another gathered around the two. Some said one thing, some another. "Poor puppet," called out a man. "I am not surprised he doesn't want to go home. Geppetto, no doubt, will beat him viciously because he is mean and cruel!"

"Geppetto looks like a good man," added another, "but with boys he's a real tyrant. If we leave that poor puppet in his hands he may tear him to pieces!" They said so much that, finally, the carabiniere ended matters by setting Pinocchio free and dragged Geppetto away to prison. The poor old fellow did not know how to defend himself, but wept and wailed like a child. Between his sobs, he said, "Ungrateful boy! To think I tried so hard to make him a well-behaved puppet! I deserve it, however! I should have

12

given the matter more thought."

What happened after this is an almost unbelievable story, but you may read it, dear readers, in the chapters to follow.

CHAPTER IV

The story of Pinocchio and the Talking Cricket, which tells how bad children do not like to be corrected by those who know more than they do

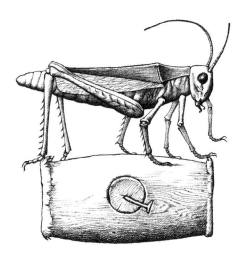

It did not take long to get poor innocent Geppetto to prison. In the meantime that rascal, Pinocchio, free now from the clutches of the carabiniere, was running wildly across fields and meadows, taking one short cut after another toward home. In his wild flight, he jumped over brambles and bushes, across brooks and over ponds, as if he were a goat or a hare chased by hounds.

On reaching home, he found the entrance partly open. He slipped into the room, locked the door, and threw himself on the floor, happy at his escape. But his happiness lasted only a short time, for just then he heard someone saying, "Crick, crick, crick!"

"Who is calling me?" asked Pinocchio, greatly frightened.

"I am!"

Pinocchio turned and saw a large cricket crawling slowly up the wall.

"Tell me, Cricket, who are you?"

"I am the Talking Cricket and I have been living in this room for more than one hundred years."

"Today, however, this room is mine," said the puppet, "and if you wish to do me a favor, get out now, and don't turn around even once."

"I refuse to leave this spot," answered the Cricket, "until I have told you a great truth."

"Tell it, then, and hurry."

"Woe to boys who disobey parents and run away from home! They will never be happy in this world, and when they are older they will be very sorry for it."

"Sing on, my dear Cricket, as you please. What I know is that tomorrow, at dawn, I leave this place forever. If I stay here the same thing will happen to me that happens to all other boys and girls. They are sent to school, and whether they want to or not, they must study. As for me, let me tell you, I hate to study! It's much more fun, I think, to chase butterflies, climb trees, and steal bird nests."

"Poor little silly! Don't you know if you go on like that, you will grow into a perfect donkey and you'll be the laughingstock of everyone?"

"Keep still, you ugly Cricket!" cried Pinocchio.

The Cricket was a wise old philosopher and, instead of being offended at Pinocchio's impudence, he continued in the same tone, "If you do not like going to school, why don't you at least learn a trade, so you can earn an honest living?"

"May I tell you something?" asked Pinocchio, who was beginning to lose his patience. "Of all the trades in the world, there is only one that really suits me."

"And what can that be?"

"That of eating, drinking, sleeping, playing, and lazing around from morning until night."

"Let me tell you, for your own good, Pinocchio," said the Talking Cricket in his calm voice, "those who follow that trade always end up in the hospital or in prison."

"Careful, ugly Cricket! If you make me angry, you'll be sorry!"

"Poor Pinocchio, I am sorry for you."

"Why?"

"Because you are a puppet and, what is much worse, you have a wooden head."

Hearing this answer, Pinocchio jumped up in a fury, took a hammer from the bench, and threw it with all his strength at the Talking Cricket. Perhaps he did not think he would strike it, but sad to relate, my dear readers, he did hit the Cricket, straight on its head. With a last weak "Crick, crick, crick" the poor Cricket fell from the wall, dead!

CHAPTER V

*Pinocchio is hungry and looks for an egg to cook an omelet but, to his
surprise, the omelet flies out the window*

If the Cricket's death scared Pinocchio at all, it was
only for a very few moments. For, as night came on,
a strange, empty feeling at the pit of his stomach
reminded the puppet that he had not eaten anything. A boy's appetite grows very fast, and in a few
moments, the strange, empty feeling had become
hunger. The hunger grew bigger and bigger, until
soon he was as ravenous as a bear.

Poor Pinocchio ran to the fireplace where the
pot was boiling and stretched out his hand to take
off the lid, but to his amazement that pot was only
a painting! Think how he felt! His long nose became at least two inches longer. He ran
about the room, dug in all the boxes and drawers, and even looked under the bed in
search of a piece of bread, hard though it might be, or a cookie, or perhaps a bit of fish.
A bone left by a dog would have tasted good to him, but he found nothing.

Meanwhile his hunger grew and grew. The only relief poor Pinocchio had was to
yawn, and he certainly did yawn. It was such a big yawn that his mouth stretched out
to the tips of his ears. Soon he became dizzy and faint. He wept and wailed to himself,
"The Talking Cricket was right. It was wrong of me to disobey my father and run away
from home. If he were here now, I wouldn't be so hungry! Oh, how horrible it is to be
hungry!"

Suddenly, he saw, among the sweepings in a corner, something round and white that
looked like a chicken's egg. At the same instant, he pounced on it. It was an egg! The
puppet's joy knew no bounds. It is impossible to describe. You must
picture it yourself. Certain that he was dreaming, he turned the egg over and over in
his hands, played with it, kissed it, and said teasingly, "And now, how will I cook you?
Should I make an omelet? No, it is better to fry you, or will I drink you? No, the best
way is to fry you in a pan. You will taste better."

No sooner said than done. He placed a pan over a brazier filled with hot coals. In
the pan, instead of oil or butter, he poured a little water. As soon as the water started
to boil . . . *crack* . . . he broke the eggshell. Instead of the white and the yolk of an egg,

out escaped a little yellow chick, fluffy and happy and smiling. Bowing politely to Pinocchio, he said to him, "Many, many thanks, indeed, Signor Pinocchio, for having saved me the trouble of breaking my shell! Goodbye and good luck to you and remember me to the family!" With these words he spread his wings and darted to the open window. Then he flew away until he disappeared into the sky.

The poor puppet stood dumbfounded, with wide eyes and an open mouth, holding the empty halves of the eggshell in his palms. When he regained his senses, he began to cry and shriek at the top of his lungs, stamping his feet on the ground and wailing all the while, "The Talking Cricket was right! If I had not run away from home and if father were here now, I should not be dying of hunger. Oh, how horrible it is to be hungry!"

His stomach kept grumbling more than ever and he had nothing to quiet it down. Then he thought of going for a walk to the nearby village, in the hope of finding some charitable person who might give him a bit of bread.

CHAPTER VI

*Pinocchio falls asleep with his feet on a brazier, and awakens the next
day with his feet all burned off*

Pinocchio hated dark streets, but in spite of it, he
was so hungry that he ran out of the house. The
night was pitch black. It was thundering and bright
flashes of lightning now and again shot across the
sky, turning it into a sea of fire. An angry wind
blew cold and raised thick clouds of dust, and all
the trees in the countryside shook and moaned.

Pinocchio was very afraid of thunder and lightning, but the hunger he felt was far greater than his
fear. In a dozen leaps and bounds, he came to the
village, completely tired out, panting like a dog.

The entire village was dark and deserted. The stores were closed, and every door and
window was shut. In the streets, not even a dog was to be seen. It seemed like the
village of the dead.

In desperation, Pinocchio ran up to a doorway and flung himself against the door-
knocker. He pulled it wildly, thinking, "Someone will surely answer that!" He was
right. An old man in a nightcap opened the window and looked out. He called down
angrily, "What do you want at this hour of night?"

"Will you be good enough to give me a piece of bread? I am very hungry."

"Wait a minute and I'll come right back," answered the old man. He thought he had
encountered one of those boys who enjoyed gallivanting around at night and ringing
doorknockers while those inside slept peacefully.

After a minute or two, the old man cried, "Get under the window and hold out your
hat!" Pinocchio had no hat, but he managed to get under the window just in time to
feel a shower of icy cold water pour down over his poor wooden head and all the rest
of him.

He returned home wet as a rag and was tired out from weariness and hunger. He no
longer had any strength to stand, so he sat down on a little stool and put his feet on
the brazier to dry them. There he fell asleep, and while he slept, his wooden feet began
to burn. Slowly, very slowly, they blackened and turned to ashes.

Pinocchio snored away happily as if his feet were not his own. At dawn, he opened

his eyes just as a loud knocking sounded at the door.

"Who is it?" he called, yawning and rubbing his eyes.

"It is me," answered a voice.

It was the voice of Geppetto.

CHAPTER VII

Geppetto returns home and gives his own breakfast to the puppet

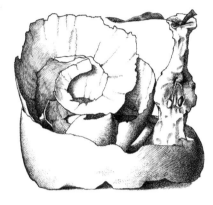

The poor puppet, still sleepy, was not aware that his feet were burned to ashes. As soon as he heard his father's voice, he jumped to open the door and staggered headlong to the floor. He fell down, making as much noise as a sack of wood falling from the fifth story of a house.

"Open the door for me!" Geppetto shouted from the street.

"Father, dear father, I can't," answered the puppet in despair, crying and rolling on the floor.

"Why can't you?"

"Because someone has eaten my feet."

"And who has eaten them?"

"The cat," answered Pinocchio, seeing the little animal playing with some shavings in the corner of the room.

"Open! I say," repeated Geppetto, "or I'll give you a sound whipping when I get in."

"Father, believe me, I can't stand up. Oh, dear! Oh, dear! I will have to walk on my knees all my life."

Geppetto, thinking that all these tears and cries were only another prank, climbed up the side of the house and went in through the window.

At first, he was very angry, but the sight of Pinocchio stretched out on the floor and really without feet made him feel very sad and sorrowful. He gathered Pinocchio off the floor and into his arms, and gave him hugs and kisses, while the tears ran down his cheeks "My young Pinocchio, my dear young Pinocchio! How did you burn your feet?" he asked.

"I don't know, father, but believe me, the night has been terrible and I will never forget it as long as I live. It was thundering and lightning, and I was very hungry. The Talking Cricket said to me, 'You deserve it, you were bad' and I said to him, 'Careful, Cricket.' Then he told me, 'You are a puppet and you have a wooden head' and I threw the hammer at him and killed him. It was his own fault because I didn't want to kill him. I put the pan on the coals, but the chick flew away and said, 'I'll see you again!

23

Best regards to the family!' Then my hunger grew even worse, so I went out, and an old man looked out the window and threw water on me. So I came home and put my feet on the brazier to dry because I was still hungry, and I fell asleep and now my feet are gone but my hunger isn't! Oh! Oh! Oh!" and poor Pinocchio began to scream and cry so loudly that he could be heard for miles around.

Geppetto, who had not understood anything of Pinocchio's jumbled talking except that he was hungry, felt sorry for him. He pulled three pears out of his pocket and offered them to him, saying, "These three pears were for my breakfast, but I give them to you gladly. Eat them and stop weeping."

"If you want me to eat them, please peel them for me."

"Peel them?" asked Geppetto, very much surprised. "I should never have thought, dear boy of mine, that you were so fussy and picky about your food. Bad, very bad! In this world, even as children, we must accustom ourselves to eat everything, for we never know what life may hold in store for us!"

"You may be right," answered Pinocchio, "but I will not eat the pears if they are not peeled. I don't like to eat the skins."

Good old Geppetto took out a knife, peeled the three pears, and put the skins in a row on the table.

Pinocchio ate one pear in a second and started to throw the core away, but Geppetto held his arm to stop him.

"Oh, no, don't throw it away! Everything in this world may be of some use!"

"But the core I will not eat!" cried Pinocchio angrily.

"Who knows?" repeated Geppetto calmly.

Later, the three cores were placed on the table next to the skins.

Pinocchio ate the three pears, or rather devoured them. Then he yawned deeply, and wailed, "I'm still hungry!"

"But I have no more to give you."

"Really, nothing . . . nothing?"

"I have only these three cores and these skins."

"Very well, then," said Pinocchio, "if there is nothing else I'll eat them."

At first, he made a wry face but one after another, the skins, and the cores disappeared in his mouth.

"Ah! Now I feel much better!" he said after eating the last one.

"You see," observed Geppetto, "I was right when I told you that one must not be too fussy or too picky about food. My dear, we never know what life may have in store for us!"

CHAPTER VIII

Geppetto makes Pinocchio a new pair of feet, and sells his coat to buy him an ABC book

After his hunger was satisfied, Pinocchio started to grumble and cry for a new pair of feet, but Maestro Geppetto, in order to punish him for his mischief, left him alone the entire morning. Later he said to him, "Why should I make you a pair of feet again? To see you run away from home once more?"

"I promise you," answered the puppet, sobbing, "from now on I'll be good . . ."

"Boys always promise that when they want something," said Geppetto.

"I promise to go to school every day, to study and work hard . . ."

"Boys always sing that song when they want their own way."

"But I am not like other boys! I am better than they are and I always tell the truth. I promise you, father, I'll learn a trade, and I'll be a comfort and support to you in your old age."

Geppetto, though trying to look very stern, felt his eyes fill with tears and his heart soften when he saw Pinocchio so unhappy. He said no more, but taking his tools and two pieces of wood, he set to work diligently. In less than an hour, the feet were finished: two slender, nimble little feet, strong and quick, made by the hands of an artisan.

"Close your eyes and sleep!" Geppetto then said to the puppet.

Pinocchio closed his eyes and pretended to be asleep, while Geppetto stuck the feet with a bit of glue melted in an eggshell, done so expertly that the joint could hardly be seen.

As soon as the puppet felt his new feet, he gave one leap from the table and started to skip and jump around with sheer happiness.

"To show you how grateful I am to you, father, I'll go to school now. But to go to school I need a suit of clothes."

Geppetto did not have a penny in his pocket, so he made his son a little suit of flowered paper, a pair of shoes from the bark of a tree, and a tiny cap from a bit of bread dough.

Pinocchio ran to look at himself in a bowl of water, and he felt so happy that he said proudly, "Now I look like a gentleman."

"Truly," answered Geppetto. "But remember that expensive clothes do not make the man unless they are neat and clean."

"Very true," answered Pinocchio, "but, in order to go to school, I still need something very important."

"What is it?"

"An ABC book."

"Certainly! But how will we get it?"

"That's easy. We'll go to a bookstore and buy it."

"And the money?"

"I have none."

"Neither have I," said the old man sadly.

Although he was usually a happy boy, Pinocchio became sad and despondent. When poverty reveals itself, even mischievous boys understand its meaning.

"What does it matter, after all?" cried Geppetto all at once, as he jumped up from his chair. Putting on his old coat, full of darns and patches, he ran out of the house without another word.

In a short time, he returned with an ABC book for his son, but the old coat was gone. The poor man was in his shirtsleeves and the day was freezing cold.

"Where's your coat, father?"

"I have sold it."

"Why did you sell your coat?"

"It was too warm."

Pinocchio understood the explanation instantly and, without holding back his tears, he jumped up to embrace his father's neck and kissed him again and again.

CHAPTER IX

Pinocchio sells his ABC book to pay his way into the Puppet Theater

Pinocchio hurried off to school with his new ABC book under his arm! As he walked along, his brain was busy planning hundreds of wonderful things, building hundreds of castles in the air. He said to himself, "In school today, I'll learn to read, tomorrow to write, and the day after tomorrow I'll do arithmetic. Then, clever as I'll be, I can earn a lot of money. With the first pennies I make, I'll buy father a new cloth coat. Cloth, did I say? No, it will be of gold and silver with diamond buttons. That poor man certainly deserves it because, after all, is he not in his shirtsleeves on this cold day only because he was good enough to buy a book for me? Fathers are very good to their children!"

As he talked to himself, he thought he heard sounds of pipes and drums coming from a distance: pi, pi, pi . . . pi, pi, pi . . . zum, zum, zum, zum. He stopped and listened. The sounds came from a little street that led to a small village along the shore. "What can that noise be? What a nuisance to have to go to school! Otherwise, . . ." Suddenly he was very puzzled about what to do. He felt he had to do either one thing or another. Should he go to school, or should he follow the pipes and drums?

"Today I'll follow the pipes and drums, and tomorrow I'll go to school. There's always plenty of time to go to school," decided the young rascal at last, shrugging his shoulders.

Down the street, he ran like the wind. Louder grew the sound of pipes and drums: pi, pi, pi . . . pi, pi, pi . . . pi, pi, pi . . . zum, zum, zum, zum. Suddenly, he discovered a large square with a crowd of people at the entrance of a little wooden building painted in brilliant colors. "What is that place?" Pinocchio asked a young boy near him.

"Read the poster and you'll know."

"I'd like to read it, but somehow I can't today."

"Oh, really? For your information, then, I'll read it to you. It says in flaming red letters, Great Puppet Theater."

"When did the show start?"

"It is just beginning."

"And how much does it cost to get in?"

"Four pennies."

Pinocchio, who was wild with curiosity to see inside the theater, lost all his pride and said to the boy shamelessly, "Will you give me four pennies until tomorrow?"

"I'd give them to you gladly," answered the other, making fun of him, "but just now I can't give them to you."

"For the price of four pennies, I'll sell you my coat."

"If it rains, what will I do with a coat of flowered paper? I could not take it off again."

"Do you want to buy my shoes?"

"They are only good enough to light a fire with."

"What about my hat?"

"A good bargain indeed! A cap of bread dough! The mice might come and eat it off my head!"

Pinocchio was on the edge of tears. He was about to make a final offer, but he did not have the courage. He hesitated and wondered what to do. At last, he said, "Will you give me four pennies for the book?"

"I am a boy and I buy nothing from boys," he said, with far more common sense than the puppet.

"I'll give you four pennies for your ABC book," said a rag picker standing nearby.

Right there, the book changed hands. And to think that poor old Geppetto sat at home in his shirt sleeves, shivering from the cold, having sold his coat to buy that ABC book for his son!

CHAPTER X

*The puppets recognize their brother Pinocchio, and greet him
with loud cheers, but the director, Fire Eater comes along and poor
Pinocchio almost loses his life*

Quick as a flash of lightening, Pinocchio disappeared into the Puppet Theater. Then something happened which almost caused a riot. The curtain was up and the performance had started. Harlequin and Punchinello were reciting on the stage and, as usual, they were threatening each other with sticks and blows. The theater was full of people, enjoying the spectacle and laughing uproariously at the antics of the two puppets.

The play continued for a few minutes and then suddenly, without any warning, Harlequin stopped his act. Turning toward the audience, he pointed to the rear of the orchestra, yelling wildly at the same time, "Look, look! Am I asleep or awake? Or do I really see Pinocchio there?"

"Yes, yes! It is Pinocchio!" screamed Punchinello.

"It is! It is!" shrieked Signora Rosaura, peeking in from the side of the stage.

"It is Pinocchio! It is Pinocchio!" screamed all the puppets, pouring out of the wings. "It is Pinocchio. It is our brother Pinocchio! Hurray for Pinocchio!"

"Pinocchio, come up to me!" shouted Harlequin. "Come to the arms of your wooden brothers!"

Pinocchio accepted their warm invitation and, with one leap from the back of the orchestra, bounded into the front rows. With another leap, he was on the conductor's head. With a third, he landed on the stage.

It is impossible to describe how, with shrieks of joy, warm embraces, friendly elbowing and affectionate greetings the strange company of dramatic actors received Pinocchio. It was a heartbreaking spectacle, but the audience, seeing that the play had stopped, became angry and began to yell, "The play, the play, we want the play to continue!" Their shouting was useless because the puppets, instead of continuing with their act, made twice as much of a racket as before. They lifted up Pinocchio on their shoulders and carried him around the stage in triumph.

At that very moment, the director came out of his room. His appearance was so

fearsome that a glance at him would fill one with horror. His beard was as black as coal and so long that it reached from his chin down to his feet. His mouth was as wide as an oven, his teeth like yellow fangs, his eyes, two glowing red coals, and his figure was huge and hairy. He cracked a long whip made of green snakes and the tails of black cats tails twisted together.

The unexpected arrival caused them all to hold their breaths. One could almost hear a fly go by. Those poor puppets, one and all, trembled like leaves in a storm.

"Why have you brought such commotion into my theater," the huge director asked Pinocchio, with the voice of an ogre suffering with a cold.

"Believe me, your honor, the fault was not mine."

"Enough! Be silent! I'll take care of you later."

When the play was finished, the director went to the kitchen where a big roast of lamb was slowly turning on the spit. More wood was needed to finish roasting it. He called Harlequin and Punchinello and said to them, "Bring that puppet to me! He looks as if he was made of well-seasoned wood. He'll make a good fire for this spit."

Harlequin and Punchinello hesitated a little. Frightened by a look from their master, they left the kitchen to obey him. A few minutes later they returned, carrying poor Pinocchio, who was wriggling and squirming like an eel and crying pitifully:

"Father, save me! I don't want to die! I don't want to die!"

CHAPTER XI

Fire Eater sneezes and forgives Pinocchio, who saves his friend,
Harlequin, from death

In the theater, there was great excitement. Fire Eater (since this was his real name) was very ugly, but he was far from being as bad as he looked. This he proved when he saw the poor puppet being brought to him, struggling with fear and crying, "I don't want to die! I don't want to die!" and felt sorry for him and began first to waver and then to weaken. Finally, he could not control himself any longer and gave a loud sneeze.

Harlequin, who until then had been as sad as a weeping willow, smiled happily, and leaning toward the puppet, whispered to him, "Good news, brother of mine! Fire Eater has sneezed and this is a sign that he feels sorry for you. You are saved!"

He explained that some people, whenever they were sad or sorrowful, would cry and wipe their eyes, whereas Fire Eater had the strange habit of sneezing every time he felt unhappy. That way was just as good as any other to show the kindness of his heart.

Fire Eater said to Pinocchio gruffly, "Stop crying! Your wailing gives me a stomach ache . . .aah-tchoo . . . aah-tchoo!" He finished with two more sneezes.

"Bless you!" said Pinocchio.

"Thanks! Are your father and mother still alive?" he asked him.

"My father, yes. My mother I have never known."

"Your poor father would suffer terribly if I were to use you as firewood. Poor old man! I feel sorry for him! Aah-tchoo . . . aah-tchoo . . . aah-tchoo!" He sneezed three more times, louder than ever.

"Bless you!" said Pinocchio.

"Thanks! However, I ought to be sorry for myself, too, just now. My good dinner is spoiled. I have no more wood for the fire, and the lamb is only half cooked. Never mind! In your place I'll burn some other puppet." He called, "Hey there! Officers!"

Two wooden officers appeared, long and thin as a yard of rope, wearing three-cornered hats and carrying swords. Fire Eater yelled at them in a hoarse voice, "Take Harlequin, tie him, and throw him on the fire. I want my lamb well done!"

Think how poor Harlequin felt! He was so scared that his legs doubled up under him and he fell to the floor.

Pinocchio watched the heartbreaking sight and threw himself at Fire Eater's feet. Weeping bitterly, he asked in a pitiful voice that could scarcely be heard, "Have pity, I beg of you, Signor Fire Eater!"

"There are no signori here!"

"Have pity, kind Sir!"

"There are no sirs here!"

"Have pity, your Excellency!"

On hearing himself addressed as your Excellency, the director of the Puppet Theater sat up very straight, stroked his long beard, and became suddenly kind and compassionate. He smiled proudly and said to Pinocchio, "Well, what do you want from me now, puppet?"

"I beg for mercy for my poor friend Harlequin, who has never done the least harm to anyone in his life."

"There is no mercy here, Pinocchio. I have spared you. Harlequin must burn in your place. I am hungry and my dinner must be cooked."

"In that case," said Pinocchio proudly, as he stood up and flung away his cap of bread dough and repeated, "In that case, my duty is clear. Come, officers! Tie me up and throw me on those flames. No, it is not fair for poor Harlequin, the best friend that I have in the world, to die in my place!"

These brave words, said in a piercing voice, made all the other puppets cry. Even the officers, who were made of wood also, cried like babies.

Fire Eater remained hard and cold as a piece of ice. But little by little, he softened and began to sneeze. And after four or five sneezes, he opened his arms wide and said to Pinocchio, "You are a brave boy! Come to my arms and kiss me!" Pinocchio ran to him, scurried like a squirrel up his long black beard, and gave Fire Eater a loving kiss on the tip of his nose.

"Has pardon been granted to me?" asked poor Harlequin in a voice that was hardly a breath.

"Pardon is yours!" answered Fire Eater. He sighed and wagged his head and added, "Well, tonight I will have to eat my lamb only half cooked, but beware the next time, puppets."

When the news spread about the pardon Fire Eater had given Pinocchio, the puppets ran to the stage, and, turning on all the lights, they danced and sang until dawn.

CHAPTER XII

Fire Eater gives Pinocchio five gold coins for his father, Geppetto, but the puppet meets a Fox and a Cat and follows them

The next day Fire Eater called Pinocchio aside and asked him, "What is your father's name?"

"Geppetto."

"And what is his trade?"

"He's a wood carver."

"Does he earn much?"

"He earns so much that he never has a penny in his pockets. Just think, in order to buy me an ABC book for school, he had to sell the only coat he owned, a coat so full of darns and patches that it was a pity."

"Poor man! I feel sorry for him. Here, take these five gold coins. Go, give them to him with my kindest regards."

Pinocchio, as may easily be imagined, thanked him a thousand times. He kissed each puppet in turn, even the officers, and set out on his homeward journey, feeling absolutely happy.

He had walked barely half a mile when he met a lame Fox and a blind Cat, walking together like two good friends. The lame Fox leaned on the Cat, and the blind Cat let the Fox lead him along.

"Good morning, Pinocchio," said the Fox, greeting him politely.

"How do you know my name?" asked the puppet.

"I know your father well."

"Where have you seen him?"

"I saw him yesterday standing at the door of his house."

"And what was he doing?"

"He was in his shirtsleeves, shivering from the cold."

"Poor father! But, after today, hopefully, he will suffer no longer."

"Why?"

"Because I have become a rich man."

"You, a rich man?" said the Fox, and he laughed out loud. The Cat was laughing also, but tried to hide it by stroking his long whiskers.

"There is nothing to laugh at," cried Pinocchio angrily. "I am very sorry to make your mouth water, but these, as you know, are five new gold coins," and he pulled out the gold coins that Fire Eater had given him.

When the gold tinkled cheerfully, the Fox held out his paw, which was supposed to be lame, without realizing it. At the same time, the Cat opened his eyes so wide that they looked like live coals, but he closed them again so quickly that Pinocchio did not notice.

"And may I ask," inquired the Fox, "what you are going to do with all your money?"

"First of all," answered the puppet, "I want to buy a beautiful new coat for my father, a coat of gold and silver with diamond buttons, after that, I'll buy an ABC book for myself."

"For yourself?"

"For myself. I want to go to school and study hard."

"Look at me," said the Fox. "For the silly reason of wanting to study, I have lost a paw."

"Look at me," said the Cat. "For the same foolish reason, I have lost the sight of both eyes."

At that moment, a blackbird, perched on the fence along the road, called out sharp and clear, "Pinocchio, do not listen to bad advice. If you do, you'll be sorry!"

Poor little blackbird! If only he had kept his thoughts to himself! In the blink of an eye, the Cat pounced on him and ate him, feathers and all. After eating the bird, he cleaned his whiskers, closed his eyes, and became blind once more.

"Poor blackbird!" said Pinocchio to the Cat. "Why did you kill him?"

"I killed him to teach him a lesson. He talks too much. Next time he will keep his opinions to himself."

By this time, the three companions had walked a long distance. Suddenly, the Fox stopped in his tracks and, turning to the puppet, said to him, "Do you want to double your gold coins?"

"What do you mean?"

"Do you want one hundred, a thousand, two thousand gold coins for your miserable five?"

"Yes, but how?"

"The way is very easy. Instead of returning home, come with us."

"And where will you take me?"

"To the town of Grabbafool."

Pinocchio thought a while and then said firmly, "No, I don't want to go. Home is near, and I'm going where father is waiting for me. How unhappy he must be that I have not returned! I have been a bad son, and the Talking Cricket was right when he said that a disobedient boy could not be happy in this world. I have learned this at my own expense. Even last night in the theater, when Fire Eater . . . *Brrrr*! The shivers run up and down my spine when I think of it."

"Well, then," said the Fox, "if you really want to go home, go ahead, but you'll be sorry."

"You'll be sorry," repeated the Cat.

"Think well, Pinocchio, you are turning your back on a fortune."

"On a fortune," repeated the Cat.

"Tomorrow your five gold coins will be two thousand!"

"Two thousand!" repeated the Cat.

"But how can they possibly become so many?" asked Pinocchio in wonderment.

"If I explain, then you'll know why," said the Fox. "Just outside the city of Grabbafool, there is a special place called the Field of Wonders. There you dig a hole and in it, you bury a gold piece. After covering up the hole with earth, you water it well, sprinkle a bit of salt on it, and then go to bed. During the night, the gold piece sprouts, grows, and blossoms. The next morning you find a beautiful tree loaded with gold coins."

"So, if I were to bury my five gold coins," cried Pinocchio with growing wonder, "tomorrow morning I should find . . . how many?"

"It is very simple to figure out," answered the Fox. "Why, you can figure it on your fingers! Granted that each piece gives you five hundred, multiply five hundred by five. Next morning you will find twenty-five hundred new, sparkling gold coins."

"Fine! Fine!" cried Pinocchio, dancing about with joy. "And as soon as I have them, I will keep two thousand for myself and the other five hundred I'll give to you two."

"A gift for us?" cried the Fox, pretending to be insulted. "Why, of course not!"

"Of course not!" repeated the Cat.

"We do not work for profit," answered the Fox. "We work only to make others rich."

"To make others rich!" repeated the Cat.

"What good people!" thought Pinocchio. Then forgetting about his father, the new coat, the ABC book, and all his good resolutions, he said to the Fox and to the Cat, "Let us go. I am with you."

CHAPTER XIII

The Inn of the Red Lobster

The Cat, the Fox, and the puppet walked for a very long time until finally toward evening, dead tired, they came to the Inn of the Red Lobster.

"Let us stop here a while," said the Fox, "to eat a bite and rest for a few hours. At midnight we'll start out again, for at dawn tomorrow we must be at the Field of Wonders."

They went into the Inn and all three sat down at the same table. However, not one of them was very hungry. The poor Cat felt very weak, and he was able to eat only thirty-five mullets with tomato sauce and four portions of tripe with cheese. Furthermore, because he needed strength, he had to have four more helpings of butter and cheese.

The Fox, after a great deal of coaxing, tried his best to eat a little. The doctor had put him on a diet, and he had to be satisfied with a small hare dressed with a dozen young and tender spring chickens. After the hare, he ordered some partridges, a few pheasants, a couple of rabbits, and a dozen frogs and lizards. That was all. He felt ill, he said, and could not eat another bite.

Pinocchio ate least of all. He asked for a bite of bread and a few nuts and then hardly touched them. The poor young puppet, with his mind on the Field of Wonders, was suffering from gold coin indigestion.

Supper over, the Fox said to the innkeeper, "Give us two good rooms, one for Signor Pinocchio and the other for me and my friend. Before starting out, we'll take a little nap. Remember to call us at midnight sharp, for we must continue on our journey."

"Yes, sir," answered the Innkeeper, winking in a crafty way at the Fox and the Cat, as if to say, "I understand."

As soon as Pinocchio was in bed, he fell fast asleep and began to dream. He dreamed he was in the middle of a field. The field was full of vines heavy with grapes. The grapes were none other than gold coins that tinkled merrily as they swayed in the wind. They seemed to say, "Let him take us if he wants!" Just as Pinocchio stretched out his hand

to take a handful of them, he was awakened by three loud knocks at the door. The innkeeper had come to tell him that midnight had struck.

"Are my friends ready?" the puppet asked him.

"Yes, in fact! They left two hours ago."

"Why in such a hurry?"

"Unfortunately the Cat received a telegram which said that his firstborn was suffering from chilblains and was on the point of death. He could not even wait to say goodbye to you."

"Did they pay for the supper?"

"How could they do such a thing? Being people of great refinement, they did not want to offend you so deeply as not to allow you the honor of paying the bill."

"Too bad! That offense would have been more than pleasing to me," said Pinocchio, scratching his head.

"Where did my good friends say they would wait for me?" he added.

"At the Field of Wonders, at sunrise tomorrow morning."

Pinocchio paid a gold piece for the three suppers and started on his way toward the field that was to make him a rich man.

He walked on, not knowing where he was going, for it was dark, so dark that nothing was visible. Round about him, not a leaf stirred. A few bats skimmed his nose now and again and scared him half to death. Once or twice, he shouted, "Who goes there?" and the faraway hills echoed back to him, "Who goes there? Who goes there? Who goes . . .?" As he walked, Pinocchio noticed a tiny insect glimmering on the trunk of a tree, a small creature that glowed with a pale, soft light.

"Who are you?" he asked.

"I am the ghost of the Talking Cricket," answered the small being in a faint voice that sounded as if it came from a faraway world.

"What do you want?" asked the puppet.

"I want to give you a few words of good advice. Return home and give the four gold coins you have left to your poor old father who is weeping because he has not seen you for many a day."

"Tomorrow my father will be a rich man, for these four gold coins will become two thousand."

"Don't listen to those who promise you wealth overnight, my boy. As a rule, they are either fools or swindlers! Listen to me and go home."

"But I want to go on!"

"The hour is late!"

"I want to go on."

"The night is very dark."

"I want to go on."

"The road is dangerous."

"I want to go on."

"Remember that boys who insist on having their own way, come to grief sooner or later."

"The same nonsense. Goodbye, Cricket."

"Good night, Pinocchio, and may heaven protect you from the murderers."

There was silence for a minute and the light of the Talking Cricket disappeared suddenly, just as if someone had snuffed it out. Once again, the road was plunged into darkness.

CHAPTER XIV

*Pinocchio does not listen to the good advice of the Talking Cricket
and falls into the hands of the murderers*

"Dear, oh, dear! When I come to think of it," thought the puppet, as he once more set out on his journey, "we boys are really very unlucky. Everybody scolds us, everybody gives us advice, and everybody warns us. If we were to allow it, everyone would try to be father and mother to us. Everyone, that is, even the Talking Cricket. Take me, for example. Just because I would not listen to that bothersome Cricket, who knows how many misfortunes may be awaiting me! Murderers indeed! At least I have never believed in them, nor ever will. To be sensible, I think fathers and mothers invented murderers to frighten their children from running away at night. Even if I was to meet them on the road, what does it matter? I'll just run up to them, and say, 'Well, signori, what do you want? Remember you can't fool me! Run along and mind your business.' When ordered like that, I can almost see those poor fellows running like the wind. But in case they don't run away, I can always run away myself . . ."

Pinocchio had no time to argue any longer, because he thought he heard a slight rustle among the leaves behind him. He turned to look and behold, there in the darkness stood two big black shadows, wrapped from head to foot in black sacks. The two figures leaped toward him as softly as if they were ghosts. "Here they come!" thought Pinocchio, and not knowing where to hide the gold coins, he stuck all four of them under his tongue. He had hardly taken a step to run away when they grabbed him by the arms and shouted in their deep voices to him, "Your money or your life!" With the gold coins in his mouth, Pinocchio could not say a word, so he gestured with his head and hands and body to show, as best he could, that he was only a poor puppet without a penny in his pocket.

"Come, come, less nonsense, and out with your money!" cried the two thieves in threatening voices.

Once more, Pinocchio's head and hands gestured, "I haven't a penny."

"Out with the money or you're a dead man," said the taller of the two murderers.

"Dead man," repeated the other.

"And after having killed you, we will kill your father also."

"Your father also!"

"No, no, no, not my father!" cried Pinocchio, wild with terror, but as he screamed, the gold coins tinkled together in his mouth.

"Ah, you rascal! So that's the game! You have the money hidden under your tongue. Out with it!"

Pinocchio remained as stubborn as ever.

"Don't pretend to be deaf! We'll make you spit it out straight away!"

One of them grabbed the puppet by the nose and the other by the chin, and they pulled him unmercifully from side to side in order to make him open his mouth. It was of no use. The puppet's lips might have been nailed together. His mouth would not open.

In desperation the smaller of the two murderers pulled out a long knife from his pocket, and tried to pry open Pinocchio's mouth. The puppet instantly sank his teeth into the murderer's hand, bit it off and spat it out. Imagine his surprise when he saw that it was not a hand, but a cat's paw!

Revitalized by this first victory, he swiftly freed himself from the claws of his attackers, leaped over the hedge beside the road, and ran away across the fields. His attackers ran in pursuit, like two dogs chasing a rabbit.

After running almost ten miles, Pinocchio was nearly exhausted. Perilously worn out, he climbed up a giant pine tree and sat on a branch at the top of it. The murderers tried to climb after him, but they slipped and fell back.

This setback only spurred them on to other methods. They gathered a bundle of wood, piled it around the foot of the pine, and set it alight. The next moment, the tree began to sputter and burn like a candle in the wind, and flames began to climb higher and higher. Not wishing to end his days as a roasted puppet, Pinocchio jumped quickly to the ground and scurried away, with the murderers closely after him.

The dawn was breaking when, without any warning at all, Pinocchio found a deep ditch full of dirty, muddy water blocked his path. What was there to do? With a "One, two, three!" he jumped clearly across the ditch. The murderers jumped after him, but they did not measure the distance and . . . *splash* . . . they fell straight into the middle of the pond! Pinocchio heard the plunge and felt a splash. He never stopped racing, but laughed and cried out, "Have a nice bath, signori!"

He thought they must surely be drowned and turned around to look. There they were, still following him, two somber figures in their black sacks, drenched and dripping with water.

CHAPTER XV

The murderers chase Pinocchio, catch him, and hang him to the branch
of a giant oak tree

As he ran, the puppet felt more and more certain that he would have to give himself up into the hands of his pursuers. Suddenly he saw a small cottage, gleaming white as snow, among the trees of the forest. "If I have enough breath left to reach that small house, I may be saved," he thought. Not waiting another moment, he darted swiftly through the woods, with the murderers still after him.

After a hard race of almost an hour, tired and out of breath, Pinocchio finally reached the door of the cottage and knocked. No one answered. He knocked again, harder than before. Behind him, he heard his persecutors' footsteps and heavy breathing. No one answered the door, and the same silence followed.

Knocking was of no use and Pinocchio, in despair, began to kick and bang against the door, as if he wanted to break it down. Then a window opened and a lovely girl appeared. She had blue hair and a face white as wax. Her eyes were closed and her hands crossed on her breast. In a voice so weak that it could hardly be heard, she whispered, "No one lives in this house. Everyone is dead."

"Won't you, at least, open the door for me?" pleaded Pinocchio.

"I also am dead."

"Dead? Then what are you doing at the window?"

"I am waiting for the coffin to take me away."

After she spoke, the young girl disappeared and the window closed without a sound.

"Oh, Lovely Girl with Blue Hair," cried Pinocchio, "open, I beg of you. Take pity on a poor puppet that is being chased by two murder…." He could not finish, because two powerful hands had grabbed him by the neck and the same two horrible voices growled menacingly, "Now we've got you!" The puppet felt as if he saw death flash before him. He trembled so hard that the joints of his legs rattled and the coins clattered under his tongue.

"Well," the murderers demanded, "will you open your mouth now or not? Ah! You do not answer? Very well, this time you have no choice!" They each pulled out a long, sharp knife and gave Pinocchio two strong whacks on his back. Fortunately Pinocchio was made of very hard wood and the knives broke into a thousand pieces. The murderers looked at each other in defeat, holding onto just the handles of the knives.

"I guess," said one murderer to the other, "there is nothing left to do but to hang him!"

"To hang him!" repeated the other.

They tied Pinocchio's hands behind his shoulders and slipped a noose around his neck. Then they threw the rope over the limb of a giant oak tree and strung him up high. Pleased with their work, they sat on the grass waiting for Pinocchio to give his last gasp of air. Yet after three hours, the puppet still had his eyes open, his mouth shut, and his legs kicking harder than ever.

Grown tired of waiting, the murderers called to him mockingly, "Goodbye until tomorrow. When we return in the morning, we hope you will have had the courtesy to let us find you dead and gone, with your mouth opened wide," and they went away.

A few minutes went by and a wild wind started to blow. As it shrieked and moaned, the small sufferer was blown back and forth like the hammer of a bell. The swaying made his stomach queasy and the noose choked his neck tighter and tighter. Little by little his eyes grew dimmer.

Death was creeping closer and closer but the puppet still hoped to be saved by a good soul to come and save him. No one came to his rescue. As he was about to die, he thought of his poor old father and mourned, "Oh, father, dear father! If you were only here!"

Those were his last words. He closed his eyes, opened his mouth, stretched out his legs, and hung there, as if he were dead.

CHAPTER XVI

*The Lovely Girl with Blue Hair sends for the poor puppet, puts him to
bed, and calls three doctors to tell her if Pinocchio is dead or alive*

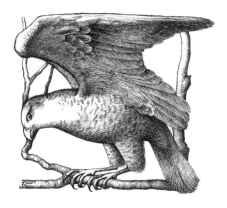

If the poor puppet had dangled there much
longer, all hope would have been lost. Luckily
for him, the Lovely Girl with Blue Hair once
more looked out of her window. Filled with
pity at the sight of the little puppet being
knocked about helplessly by the wind, she
clapped her hands sharply three times. At the
signal, there was a loud beating of wings in
flight and a large Falcon flew down and settled
on the window ledge.

"What do you command, my charming Fairy?"
asked the Falcon, lowering his beak in deep reverence (since the Lovely Girl with Blue
Hair was none other than a very kind Fairy who had lived for more than a thousand
years in the forest surroundings).

"Do you see that puppet hanging from the limb of the giant oak tree?"

"I see him."

"Very well. Fly to him immediately. With your strong beak, break the knot that ties
him, take him down, and lay him softly on the grass at the foot of the oak."

The Falcon flew away and after two minutes returned and said, "I have done what
you have commanded."

"How did you find him? Dead or alive?"

"At first glance, I thought he was dead. But I realized that I was wrong, for as soon
as I unfastened the knot around his neck, he gave a long sigh and mumbled in a faint
voice, 'Now I feel better!'"

The Fairy clapped her hands twice. A magnificent poodle appeared, walking on his
hind legs just like a man. He was dressed in court livery. A three-cornered hat trimmed
with gold lace was set at an angle over a wig of white curls that fell to his waist. He wore
a coat of chocolate color velvet, with diamond buttons, and two huge pockets that
were always filled with bones put there at dinner by his loving mistress. Breeches of
crimson velvet, silk stockings, and silver-buckled shoes completed his costume. His tail
was encased in a blue silk covering, to protect it from the rain.

50

"Come, Medoro," said the Fairy to him. "Get my best coach ready and set out toward the forest. On reaching the oak tree, you will find a poor, half-dead puppet stretched out on the grass. Lift him up tenderly, place him on the silken cushions of the coach, and bring him here to me."

The poodle wagged his silk-covered tail two or three times to show that he understood, and set off quickly.

In a few minutes, a beautiful coach appeared, made of glass with a lining of whipped cream and sponge cake and cushions padded with canary feathers. It turned out of the stable, pulled by one hundred pairs of white mice. The poodle sat proudly on the coachman's seat and cracked his whip in the air, as if he were a real driver hurrying to his destination.

In a quarter of an hour the coach was back. The Fairy, who was waiting for Pinocchio's arrival at the door of the house, lifted the poor puppet in her arms, took him to a small room with inlaid mother-of-pearl walls, put him to bed, and sent immediately for the most famous doctors of the neighborhood to come to her. One after another, the doctors arrived: a Crow, and Owl, and a Talking Cricket.

"I should like to know something, signori," said the Fairy, turning to the three doctors gathered around Pinocchio's bed, "I should like to know if this poor puppet is dead or alive."

Following this request, the Crow stepped out and felt Pinocchio's pulse, his nose, and his little toe. Then he solemnly pronounced, "To my mind this puppet is dead and gone but, if by any evil chance he were not, then it would be a sure sign that he is still alive!"

"I am sorry," said the Owl, "to have to contradict the Crow, my famous friend and colleague. To my mind this puppet is alive but if, by any evil chance, he were not, then it would be a sure sign that he is wholly dead!"

"And do you hold any opinion?" the Fairy asked the Talking Cricket.

"I say that a wise doctor, when he does not know what he is talking about, should know enough to keep his mouth shut. However, that puppet is not a stranger to me. I have known him a long time!"

Pinocchio, who had been very still, shuddered so hard that he made the bed shake.

"That puppet," continued the Talking Cricket, "is a rascal of the worst kind."

Pinocchio opened his eyes and closed them again.

"He is a rude and lazy runaway."

Pinocchio hid his face under the sheets.

"That puppet is a disobedient son who is breaking his father's heart!"

Everyone's attention turned to the sobbing and crying from under the sheets. Think of the surprise when they raised the sheets and discovered Pinocchio melting in tears!

"When the dead weep, they are beginning to recover," said the Crow solemnly.

"I am sorry to contradict my famous friend and colleague," said the Owl, "but in my view, I think that when the dead weep, it means they do not want to die."

CHAPTER XVII

*Pinocchio eats sugar, but refuses to take medicine. When the undertakers
come for him, he drinks the medicine and feels better. Afterward he tells a
lie and, in punishment, his nose grows longer and longer*

As soon as the three doctors had left the room, the Fairy went to Pinocchio's bed and, touching him on the forehead, noticed that he was burning with fever. She took a glass of water, put a white powder in it and handed it to the puppet, and said lovingly to him, "Drink this, and in a few days you'll be up and well."

Pinocchio looked at the glass, made a funny face, and asked in a whining voice, "Is it sweet or bitter?"

"It is bitter, but it is good for you."

"If it is bitter, I don't want it."

"Drink it!"

"I don't like anything bitter."

"Drink it and I'll give you a lump of sugar to take the bitter taste from your mouth."

"Where's the sugar?"

"Here it is," said the Fairy, taking a lump from a golden sugar bowl.

"I want the sugar first, then I'll drink the bitter water."

"Do you promise?"

"Yes."

The Fairy gave him the sugar and Pinocchio, after chewing and swallowing it in a moment, said, smacking his lips, "If only sugar were medicine! I should take it every day."

"Now keep your promise and drink these few drops of water. They'll be good for you."

Pinocchio took the glass in both hands and stuck his nose into it. He lifted it to his mouth and once more stuck his nose into it.

"It is too bitter, much too bitter! I can't drink it."

"How do you know, when you haven't even tasted it?"

"I can imagine it. I smell it. I want another lump of sugar, then I'll drink it."

The Fairy, with all the patience of a good mother, gave him a bit more sugar and

handed him the glass again.

"I can't drink it like that," the puppet said, making more wry faces.

"Why?"

"Because that feather pillow on my feet bothers me."

The Fairy took away the pillow.

"It's no use. I can't drink it even now."

"What's the matter now?"

"I don't like the way that door looks. It's half open."

The Fairy closed the door.

"I won't drink it," cried Pinocchio, bursting out crying. "I won't drink this awful water. I won't. I won't! No, no, no, no, no!"

"My boy, you'll be sorry."

"I don't care."

"You are very sick."

"I don't care."

"In a few hours the fever will take you far away to another world."

"I don't care."

"Aren't you afraid of death?"

"Not a bit. I'd rather die than drink that awful medicine."

At that moment, the door of the room flew open and in came four rabbits as black as ink, carrying a small black coffin on their shoulders.

"What do you want from me?" asked Pinocchio.

"We have come for you," said the largest rabbit.

"For me? But I'm not dead yet!"

"No, not dead yet but you will be in a few moments since you have refused to take the medicine which would have made you well."

"Oh, Fairy, my Fairy," the puppet cried out, "give me the glass! Quick, please! I don't want to die! No, no, not yet . . . not yet!" And holding the glass in both hands, he swallowed the medicine in one gulp.

"Well," said the four rabbits, "this time we have made the trip for nothing."

And turning on their heels, they marched solemnly out of the room, carrying their small black coffin and muttering and grumbling between their teeth.

Pinocchio felt better right away. With one leap he was out of bed and into his clothes. The Fairy, seeing him run and jump around the room, as happy as he could be, said to him, "My medicine was good for you, after all, wasn't it?"

"Very good! It has given me new life."

"Why, then, did I have to beg you so hard to make you drink it?"

"I'm a boy, you see, and all boys hate taking medicine more than they do feeling sick."

"What a shame! Boys ought to know that, after all, medicine might save them from suffering and even from death."

"Next time I won't make such a fuss. I'll remember those black rabbits with the black coffin on their shoulders and I'll take the glass and *pouf*, down it will go!"

"Come here now and tell me how it happened that you came into the hands of the murderers."

"Fire Eater gave me five gold coins to give to my father, but on the way, I met a Fox and a Cat, who asked me, 'Do you want the five coins to become two thousand?' And I said, 'Yes.' And they said, 'Come with us to the Field of Wonders.' And I said, 'Let's go.' Then they said, 'Let us stop at the Inn of the Red Lobster for dinner and after midnight we'll set out again.' We ate and went to sleep. When I awoke they were gone and I started out in the darkness all by myself.

"On the road I met two murderers dressed in black coal sacks, who said to me, 'Your money or your life!' and I said, 'I haven't any money' because, you see, I had put the money under my tongue. One of them tried to put his hand in my mouth and I bit it off and spat it out, but it wasn't a hand, it was a cat's paw. And they ran after me and I ran and ran, until at last they caught me and tied my neck with a rope and hung me from a tree. And they said, 'Tomorrow we'll come back for you and you'll be dead and your mouth will be open, and then we'll take the gold coins that you have hidden under your tongue.'"

"Where are the gold coins now?" the Fairy asked.

"I lost them," answered Pinocchio, but he told a lie, for he had them in his pocket. As he spoke, his nose, long though it was, became at least two inches longer.

"And where did you lose them?"

"In the forest nearby."

After this second lie, his nose grew a few more inches.

"If you lost them in the forest nearby," said the Fairy, "we'll look for them and find them, for everything that is lost there is always found."

"Ah, I just remembered," replied the Pinocchio, who was getting things mixed up a little. "I did not lose the gold coins. I swallowed them when I drank the medicine."

After this third lie, his nose became longer than ever, so long that he could not even turn around. If he turned to the right, he knocked it against the bed, or into the windowpanes. If he turned to the left, he struck the walls or the door. If he raised it a bit, he almost put the Fairy's eyes out. The Fairy sat looking at him and laughing.

"Why do you laugh?" the puppet asked her, worried now at the sight of his growing nose.

"I am laughing at your lies."

"How do you know I am lying?"

"Lies, my boy, are known in a moment. There are two kinds of lies, lies with short legs and lies with long noses. Yours, just now, happen to have long noses."

Pinocchio, not knowing where to hide his shame, tried to escape from the room, but his nose had become so long that he could not get it through the door.

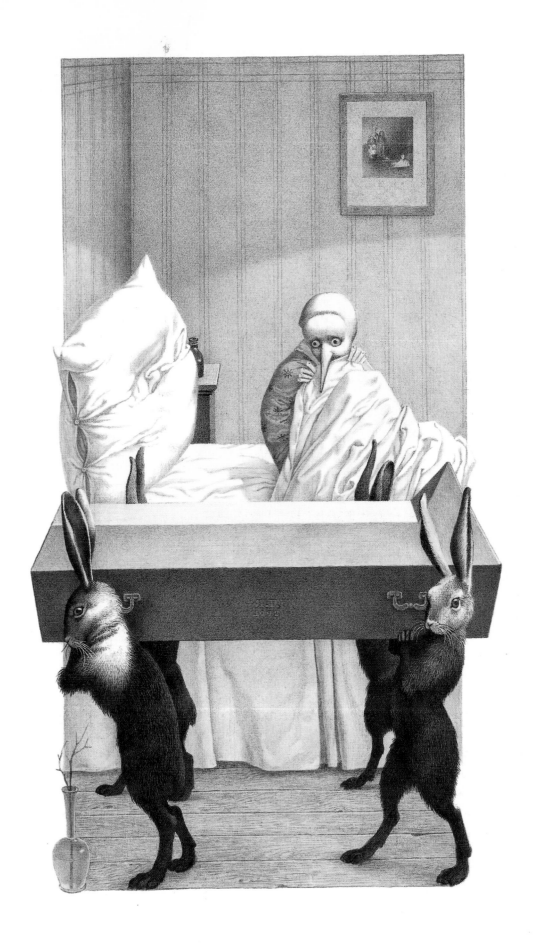

CHAPTER XVIII

Pinocchio finds the Fox and the Cat again, and goes with them to sow the gold coins in the Field of Wonders

Crying as if his heart would break, the puppet mourned for hours over the length of his nose. No matter how hard he tried, it would not go through the door. The Fairy showed no pity toward him. She was trying to teach him a good lesson, so that he would stop telling lies; the worst habit any boy may acquire. But when she saw him pale with terror and in such despair, she began to feel sorry for him. Clapping her hands together, a thousand woodpeckers flew in through the window and settled upon Pinocchio's nose. They pecked and pecked very hard at his enormous nose. In a few minutes, it was just the same size as normal.

"How good you are, my Fairy," said Pinocchio, drying his eyes, "and how much I love you!"

"I love you, too," answered the Fairy, "and if you wish to stay with me, you may be my little brother and I'll be your good little sister."

"I should like to stay . . . but what about my poor father?"

"I have thought of everything. Your father has been sent for and before nightfall he will be here."

"Really?" cried Pinocchio joyfully. "Then, my good Fairy, if you are willing, I should like to go to meet him. I cannot wait to kiss that dear old man, who has suffered so much for my sake."

"Go ahead then, but be careful not to lose your way. Take the forest path and you'll surely meet him."

Pinocchio set out, and as soon as he was in the forest, he ran like a hare. When he reached the giant oak tree he stopped, for he thought he heard a rustle in the bushes. He was right. There appeared the Fox and the Cat, the two traveling companions with whom he had eaten at the Inn of the Red Lobster.

"Here comes our dear Pinocchio!" cried the Fox, hugging and kissing him. "How did you get here?"

"How did you get here?" repeated the Cat.

"It is a long story," said the puppet. "Let me tell it to you. The other night, when you left me alone at the Inn, I met the murderers on the road . . . ."

"The murderers? Oh, my poor friend! And what did they want?"

"They wanted my gold coins."

"Rascals!" said the Fox.

"The worst sort of rascals!" added the Cat.

"But I began to run," continued the puppet, "and they ran after me, until they overtook me and hanged me to the branch of that oak tree." Pinocchio pointed to the giant oak nearby.

"Could anything be worse?" said the Fox.

"What an awful world to live in! Where will we find a safe place for gentlemen like ourselves?"

As the Fox talked like that, Pinocchio noticed the Cat was carrying his right paw in a sling. "What happened to your paw?" he asked. The Cat tried to answer, but he became so terribly confused that the Fox had to help him out.

"My friend is too modest to answer. I'll answer for him. About an hour ago, we met an old wolf on the road. He was half starved and begged for help. Having nothing to give him, what do you think my friend did out of the kindness of his heart? He bit off the paw of his front foot and threw it at the poor beast, so that he might have something to eat." As he spoke, the Fox wiped away a tear. Pinocchio, who was almost in tears, whispered in the Cat's ear, "If all cats were like you, how lucky mice would be!"

"And what are you doing here?" the Fox asked the puppet.

"I am waiting for my father, who will be here at any moment."

"And where are your gold coins?"

"I still have them in my pocket, except the one I spent at the Inn of the Red Lobster."

"To think that those four gold coins might become two thousand tomorrow. Why don't you listen to me? Why don't you plant them in the Field of Wonders?"

"Today it is impossible. I'll go with you some other time."

"Another day will be too late," said the Fox.

"Why?"

"Because the field has been bought by a very rich man, and today is the last day it will be open to the public."

"How far is this Field of Wonders?"

"Only two miles away. Will you come with us? We'll be there in half an hour. You can plant the money, and, after a few minutes, you can gather your two thousand coins and return home rich. Are you coming?"

Pinocchio hesitated before answering, because he remembered the good Fairy, old Geppetto, and the advice of the Talking Cricket. Then he ended by doing what all boys do, when they have no heart and a small brain. He shrugged his shoulders and said to the Fox and the Cat, "Let us go! I am with you." And away they went.

They walked and walked for a half a day at least and at last they came to the town called Grabbafool. As soon as he entered the town, Pinocchio noticed that all the streets were filled with mangy dogs, yawning from hunger, fleeced sheep, trembling with cold, chickens without their crests, begging for a grain of wheat, large butterflies, unable to fly because they had sold their beautiful wings, peacocks without tails, ashamed to display themselves, and bedraggled pheasants, scuttling away hurriedly, grieving for their bright feathers of gold and silver, lost to them forever.

Through this crowd of paupers and beggars, a beautiful coach passed now and again. Inside sat a fox, a hawk, or a vulture. "Where is the Field of Wonders?" asked Pinocchio, growing tired of waiting.

"Be patient. It is only a few more steps away."

They passed through the city and beyond its walls they stepped into a lonely field that looked, more or less, like any other field.

"Here we are," said the Fox to the puppet. "Dig a hole here and put the gold coins into it." The puppet obeyed. He dug the hole, put the four gold coins into it, and covered them up very carefully. "Now," said the Fox, "go to that nearby brook, bring back a pail full of water, and sprinkle it over the spot." Pinocchio followed the directions closely, but, as he had no pail, he pulled off his shoe, filled it with water, and sprinkled the earth covering the gold. Then he asked, "Anything else?"

"Nothing else," answered the Fox. "Now we can go. Return here within twenty minutes and you will find the vine has grown and its branches filled with gold coins."

Pinocchio, feeling overcome with joy, thanked the Fox and the Cat many times and promised them each a beautiful gift. "We don't want any of your gifts," answered the two rascals. "It is enough for us that we have helped you to become rich with little or no trouble. For this we are as happy as kings."

They said goodbye to Pinocchio and wished him good luck, and went on their way.

CHAPTER XIX

Pinocchio is robbed of his gold coins and, in punishment, is sentenced to four months in prison

The puppet went back to the town and began to count the minutes one by one. Finally he turned toward the Field of Wonders. As he walked hurriedly, his heart beat with an excited tick tock, tick tock, just like a clock. His busy brain kept wondering, "What if, instead of a thousand, I should find two thousand? And what if, instead of two thousand, I should find five thousand . . . or one hundred thousand? I would want to have a beautiful palace, with a thousand stables filled with a thousand wooden horses to play with, a cellar overflowing with lemonade and ice cream soda, and a huge assortment of candies and fruits, cakes and cookies." Amusing himself with these ideas, he came to the field.

There he stopped to see if, by any chance, a vine filled with gold coins was in sight. But he saw nothing! He took a few steps forward, and still nothing! He stepped into the field. He went up to the place where he had dug the hole and buried the gold coins. Again nothing! Pinocchio became very pensive and, forgetting his good manners altogether, drew a hand from his pocket and stood scratching his head thoughtfully. As he did so, he heard a hearty burst of laughter close to his head. He turned sharply, and there, just above him on the branch of a tree, sat a large Parrot, busily preening his feathers.

"What are you snickering at?" Pinocchio asked irritably.

"I am just laughing because, while preening my feathers, I tickled myself under the wings."

The puppet did not reply. He walked to the brook, filled his shoe with water, and once more sprinkled the ground covering the gold coins.

Another burst of laughter, even more disparaging than the first, was heard in the quiet field.

"Well," cried the puppet, angrily this time, "may I know, you ignorant Parrot, what you find so funny?"

"I am laughing at those blockheads who believe everything they hear and who allow themselves to be caught so easily in the traps set for them."

"Do you, perhaps, mean me?"

"I certainly do mean you, poor Pinocchio . . . you are one such fool to believe that gold can be sown in a field just like beans or squash. I believed it too, and today I am very sorry for it. Today, when it is too late, I have reached the conclusion that one must work and know how to earn money honestly, with one's hands or one's brain."

"I don't know what you are talking about," said the puppet, who was beginning to tremble with fear.

"Too bad! I'll explain myself better," said the Parrot. "While you were away in the city the Fox and the Cat returned here in a great hurry. They took the four gold coins you had buried and ran away as fast as the wind. If you can catch them, you're a brave one!"

Pinocchio's mouth opened wide. He could not believe what the Parrot said and began to dig away furiously at the earth. He dug and he dug until the hole was as big as he was, but there was no money was there. Every coin was gone.

In a panic, he ran to the city and went straight to the courthouse to report the robbery to the magistrate. The judge was an elder Gorilla of a venerable age, with a flowing white beard covering his chest and wearing gold-rimmed spectacles from which the glasses had dropped out. The reason for wearing them, he said, was that his eyes had been weakened by the work of many years.

Pinocchio, standing before him, told his tragic story, word by word. He gave the names and the descriptions of the robbers and begged for justice. The judge listened to him with great patience and sympathy. He became absorbed in the story. He was moved and deeply touched. When the puppet had no more to say, the judge put out his hand and rang a bell.

The bell summoned two large mastiffs that appeared before the judge, dressed in the uniform of the carabinieri. Then the judge, pointing to Pinocchio, said in a very solemn voice, "This poor pathetic soul has been robbed of four gold coins. Therefore, take him and throw him into prison."

The puppet, on hearing this sentence passed upon him, was thoroughly stupefied. He tried to protest, but the two officers clapped their paws on his mouth and hustled him away to jail.

There he was imprisoned for four long, weary months. If it had not been for a stroke of luck, he probably would have had to stay there longer. For, my dear readers, be aware of what happened around that same time. When the young emperor who ruled over the town of Grabbafool won a great victory over his enemies, he ordered civic illuminations, fireworks, and festivals of all kinds to celebrate his triumph. Best of all, he ordered the opening of all the prison doors and all the scoundrels set free.

"If the others go, I go, too," said Pinocchio to the jailer.

"Not you," answered the jailer. "You aren't included."

"I beg your pardon," interrupted Pinocchio, "I am a scoundrel, too."

"In that case you are also set free," said the jailer. Taking off his cap, he bowed deeply and opened the prison door for Pinocchio, who ran out and away, without looking backward.

CHAPTER XX

*Freed from prison, Pinocchio sets out to return to the Fairy, but on the way
he meets a Serpent and later is caught in a trap*

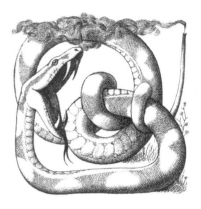

Imagine how happy Pinocchio felt to be free
again! Without saying yes or no, he fled from the
city and set out on the road that would to take
him back to the house of the lovely Fairy.

It had rained for many days, and the road had
become so muddy that, at times, Pinocchio sank
down almost to his knees. But he kept on bravely.
Tormented by the wish to see his father and his
fairy sister with blue hair, he raced like a grey-
hound. As he ran, he was splattered with mud all
the way to his cap.

"How unhappy I have been," he thought. "And yet I deserve everything, for I am
certainly very stubborn and stupid! I will always have my own way. I won't listen to
those who love me and who have more brains than I do. But from now on, I'll be
different and I'll try to become a most obedient boy. I have learned beyond any doubt
that disobedient boys are certainly far from happy and in the long run, they always lose
out. I wonder if father is waiting for me. Will I find him at the Fairy's house? It is so
long, poor man, since I have seen him, and I do so want his love and his kisses. And
will the Fairy ever forgive me for all I have done? She who has been so good to me and
to whom I owe my life! Can there be a worse or a more heartless boy than I am anywhere?" As he spoke, he stopped suddenly, frozen with terror. What was the matter?

An immense Serpent lay stretched across the road. A Serpent with bright green skin,
fiery eyes that glowed and burned, and a pointed tail that smoked like a chimney. How
it frightened poor Pinocchio! He ran back wildly for half a mile and settled himself at
last on a heap of stones to wait for the Serpent to go on his way and leave the road clear
for him.

He waited an hour, two hours, three hours, but the Serpent remained. Even from a
distance, one could see the flash of his red eyes and the column of smoke rising from
his long, pointed tail. Pinocchio, trying to feel very brave, walked straight up to him
and said in a sweet, soothing voice, "I beg your pardon, Signor Serpent, but would you
be so kind as to move aside to let me pass?" He might as well have talked to a wall. The

Serpent never budged.

Once more, in the same sweet voice, he spoke, "May I tell you, Signor Serpent, that I am going home and my father is waiting for me. It is so long since I have seen him! Would you mind very much if I passed?"

He waited for some sign of an answer to his questions, but the answer did not come. On the contrary, the Serpent, which had seemed alert and lively until then, became suddenly very quiet and still. His eyes closed and his tail stopped smoking.

"Is he dead, I wonder?" said Pinocchio, rubbing his hands together happily. Without a moment's hesitation, he started to step over him, but just as he had lifted a leg, the Serpent sprang up again and the puppet fell head over heels backward. He fell so clumsily that he plunged headfirst into the mire and was stuck upside down, with his legs straight up in the air. At the sight of the puppet kicking and twisting like a tornado, the Serpent convulsed into such an unstoppable fit of laughter that he burst an artery in his heart and died on the spot.

Pinocchio managed to put himself right and ran away in search of the Fairy's house, hoping to reach it before dark. Along the way, his hunger pangs grew unendurable. Spying some tempting looking grapes, he jumped into a field to pick a few. Sorry for Pinocchio! No sooner had he reached the grapevine than *crack* went his legs!

The poor puppet was caught in a trap set there by a farmer for some weasels that came every night to steal his chickens.

CHAPTER XXI

Pinocchio is caught by a farmer, who uses him as a watchdog for his chicken coop

Pinocchio, as you may well imagine, began to scream and weep and beg, but it was of no use, for no houses were to be seen and not a soul passed by on the road. Finally, nighttime arrived. A little because the trap gave him a sharp pain in his legs, and a little because he was frightened to be alone in the darkness, the puppet was about to faint when he saw a tiny Firefly fluttering by. He called to her and said, "Dear little Firefly, will you set me free?"

"Poor little one!" replied the Firefly, stopping to look at him lamentably. "How did you get caught in this trap?"

"I stepped into this lonely field to take a few grapes and . . ."

"Are the grapes yours?"

"No."

"Who taught you to take things that do not belong to you?"

"I was hungry."

"Hunger, my boy, is no excuse for taking something which belongs to another."

"It's true, it's true!" cried Pinocchio in tears. "I won't do it again!"

Just then, approaching footsteps interrupted their conversation. It was the owner of the field, who was sneaking along, hoping to see if he had caught the weasels, which had been eating his chickens. Great was his amazement when he held up his lantern and saw that, instead of a weasel, he had caught a boy!

"Ah ha, you little thief!" said the farmer angrily. "So you are the one who steals my chickens!"

"Not I! No, no!" protested Pinocchio, sobbing bitterly. "I only came here to take a few grapes!"

"He who steals grapes may very easily steal chickens also. Take my word for it, I'll give you a lesson that you'll remember for a long time." He opened the trap, grabbed the puppet by the scruff of his neck, and carried him to the house like as if he were a baby lamb. When he reached the yard, he flung him to the ground, put a foot on his neck, and said to him roughly, "It is late and time for bed. Tomorrow we'll settle matters. In the meantime, since my watchdog died today, you may take his place and guard my chicken coop."

No sooner had he said that had he slipped a dog collar around Pinocchio's neck and fastened it tightly. A long iron chain was tied to the collar, and the other end was nailed to the wall. "If it should happen to rain tonight," said the farmer, "you can sleep in that doghouse nearby, where you will find plenty of straw for a soft bed. It has been Melampo's bed for three years, and it will be good enough for you. And if, by any chance, any thieves should come, be sure to bark!" After this last warning, the farmer went into the house and closed the door and barred it.

Poor Pinocchio huddled close to the doghouse more dead than alive from cold, hunger, and fright. Now and again he pulled and tugged at the collar that nearly choked him and cried out in a weak voice, "I deserve it! Yes, I deserve it! I have been nothing but a truant and a vagrant. I have never obeyed anyone and I have always done as I pleased. If only I were like others and had studied and worked and stayed with my poor old father, I should not find myself here now, in this field, in the darkness, replacing a farmer's watchdog. Oh, if I could start all over again! But what is done can't be undone and I must stay calm about it!"

After this short speech, which came from the very depths of his heart, Pinocchio went into the doghouse and fell asleep.

CHAPTER XXII

*Pinocchio discovers the thieves and, as a reward for faithfulness, he
regains his liberty*

Even though a boy may be very unhappy, he very
seldom loses sleep over his worries. The puppet,
being no exception to this rule, slept on peacefully for a few hours until well toward midnight,
when he was awakened by strange whisperings
and stealthy sounds coming from the yard. He
stuck his nose out of the doghouse and saw four
slender, hairy animals. They were the weasels,
small animals that like to eat chickens and their
eggs. One of them left her companions and went
to the door of the doghouse and said tenderly,
"Good evening, Melampo."

"My name is not Melampo," answered Pinocchio.

"Who are you, then?"

"I am Pinocchio."

"What are you doing here?"

"I'm the watchdog."

"But where is Melampo? Where is the old dog who used to live in this house?"

"He died this morning."

"Died? Poor beast! He was so good! Still, judging by your face, I think you are a
good-natured dog, too."

"I beg your pardon, I am not a dog!"

"What are you, then?"

"I am a puppet."

"Are you replacing the watchdog?"

"I'm sorry to say that I am. I'm being punished."

"Well, I will make the same terms with you that we had with the dead Melampo. I
am sure you will be glad to hear them."

"And what are the terms?"

"This is our plan. We will come once in a while, as in the past, to pay a visit to this
chicken coop, and we'll take away eight chickens. Of these, seven are for us, and one

for you, provided, of course, you will pretend to be asleep and will not bark for the farmer."

"Did Melampo really do that?" asked Pinocchio.

"Yes, in fact he did, and because of that we were the best of friends. Sleep away peacefully, and remember that, before we go, we will leave you a nice fat chicken all ready for your breakfast in the morning. Is that understood?"

"Even too well," answered Pinocchio. Shaking his head in a disgusted way, he seemed to say, "We'll soon see about that, my friends."

As soon as the four weasels had talked things over, they went straight to the chicken coop that stood close to the doghouse. Digging busily with their teeth and claws, they opened the little door and slipped in. But soon as they were inside, they heard the door close with a sharp bang. The one who delivered the slam was Pinocchio who, still not satisfied, dragged a heavy stone in front of the door to secure it. When he was finished, he started to bark. He barked as if he were a real watchdog, "Bow, wow, wow! Bow, wow!"

The farmer heard the loud barks and jumped out of bed. Taking his gun, he leaped to the window and shouted, "What's the matter?"

"The thieves are here!" answered Pinocchio.

"Where are they?"

"In the chicken coop."

"I'll come down in a second."

And, in fact, he was down in the yard in an instant and running toward the chicken coop.

He opened the door, pulled out the weasels one by one, and, after tying them in a sack, said to them in a happy voice, "You're in my hands at last! I could punish you now, but I'll wait! In the morning you may come with me to the inn and there you'll make a tasty dinner for some hungry mortal. It is really too great an honor for you, one you do not deserve but, as you see, I am really a very kind and generous man and I am going to do this for you!" Then he went up to Pinocchio and gave him a warm and affectionate pat.

"How did you ever find them out so quickly? And to think that Melampo, my faithful Melampo, never had an encounter with them in all these years!"

The puppet could have told, then and there, all he knew about the shameful contract between the dog and the weasels, but thinking of the dead dog, he considered, "Melampo is dead. What is the use of accusing him? The dead are gone and have no defense. The best thing to do is to leave them in peace!"

"Were you awake or asleep when they came?" continued the farmer.

"I was asleep," answered Pinocchio, "but they woke me with their rustling. One of them even came to the door of the doghouse and said to me, 'If you promise not to bark, we will make you a present of one of the chickens for your breakfast.' Did you hear that? They had the audacity to make such a proposition to me! I admit, although

74

I am a very wicked puppet full of faults, still I never have been, nor ever will be, bribed."

"Good boy!" cried the farmer, slapping him on the shoulder in a friendly way. "You ought to be proud of yourself. And to show you what I think of you, you are free this instant!" And he slipped the dog collar from his neck.

CHAPTER XXIII

*Pinocchio weeps upon learning that the Lovely Girl with Blue Hair is
dead. He meets a Pigeon, which carries him to the seashore. He throws
himself into the sea to go to the aid of his father*

As soon as Pinocchio no longer felt the shameful
weight of the dog collar around his neck, he
started to run across the fields and meadows, and
never stopped until he came to the main road
that would take him to the Fairy's house.

When he reached the main road, a view of the
valley spread out before him. He saw where he
had unluckily met the Fox and the Cat in the
forest and the tall oak tree where he had been
hanged but, although he searched far and
wide, he could not see the house belonging to the
Fairy with the Blue Hair.

He felt terribly frightened and ran as fast as he could until he finally came to the spot
where it had once stood. The small house was no longer there. Where the house had
stood lay a small marble slab, with a mournful inscription. He read:

HERE LIES
THE LOVELY FAIRY WITH BLUE HAIR
WHO DIED OF GRIEF
WHEN ABANDONED BY
HER LITTLE BROTHER PINOCCHIO

The poor puppet was heartbroken at reading these words. He fell to the ground and,
covering the cold marble with kisses, dissolved into tears of sadness, and cried all
night. By dawn his tears were dried up, but he still moaned and sobbed so loudly that
he could be heard in the faraway hills.

In the midst of sobbing, he cried, "Oh, my Fairy, my dear, dear Fairy, why did you
die? Why did I not die, who am so bad, instead of you, who are so good? And my father
. . . where can he be? Please dear Fairy, tell me where he is and I will never, never leave
him again! You are not really dead, are you? If you love me, you will come back, alive
as before. Don't you feel sorry for me? I'm so lonely. If the two murderers come, they'll

hang me again from the giant oak tree, and I will really die this time. What will I do alone in the world? Now that you are dead and my father is lost, where will I eat? Where will I sleep? Who will buy my new clothes? Oh, I want to die! Yes, I want to die! Oh, oh, oh!"

Poor Pinocchio! He even tried to tear his hair, but as it was only painted on his wooden head, he could not even pull at it. Just then a large Pigeon flew far above him. Seeing the puppet, he cried out, "Tell me lad, what are you doing there?"

"Can't you see? I'm crying," cried Pinocchio, lifting his head toward the voice and rubbing his eyes with his sleeve.

"Tell me," asked the Pigeon, "do you by chance know of a puppet, Pinocchio by name?"

"Pinocchio! Did you say Pinocchio?" replied the puppet, jumping to his feet. "Why, I am Pinocchio!"

On hearing this news, the Pigeon flew down swiftly down to the earth. For a Pigeon, he was even larger than a turkey.

"Then you know Geppetto also?"

"Do I know him? He's my father, my poor, dear father! Has he, perhaps, spoken to you of me? Will you take me to him? Is he still alive? Answer me, please! Is he still alive?"

"I left him three days ago on the seashore."

"What was he doing?"

"He was building a small boat to sail across the ocean. For the last four months, the poor man has been wandering everywhere throughout Europe, looking for you. Because he could not find you, he has decided to go far away in order to look for you in the New World."

"How far is it from here to the seashore?" asked Pinocchio anxiously.

"More than fifty miles."

"Fifty miles? Oh, dear Pigeon, how I wish I had your wings!"

"If you want to come, I'll take you with me."

"How?"

"Astride my back. Are you very heavy?"

"Heavy? No, I'm as light a feather."

"Very well then."

Saying nothing more, Pinocchio jumped on the Pigeon and, as he settled upon his back, he cried out happily, "Gallop on, gallop on, my little horse! I'm in a big hurry."

The Pigeon flew away, and in a few minutes he had reached the clouds. The puppet looked to see what was below them. He felt so dizzy and scared that he clutched the Pigeon's neck to keep himself from falling.

They flew all day. Toward the evening the Pigeon said, "I'm very thirsty!"

"And I'm very hungry!" said Pinocchio.

"Let us stop a few minutes at that dovecote down there. Then we will continue onward and be at the seashore in the morning."

They went into the empty dovecote and there they found nothing but a bowl of water and a small basket filled with chickling. The puppet had always hated chickling. According to him, it always made him sick, but that night he ate it with gusto. After he finished eating, he turned to the Pigeon and said, "I never should have thought that chickling could be so good!"

"You must remember, my boy," answered the Pigeon, "hunger sharpens the appetite!"

After resting a few minutes longer, they set out again. The next morning they were at the seashore. Pinocchio jumped off the Pigeon's back, and the Pigeon, not wanting any thanks for a kind deed, flew away swiftly, and disappeared.

The shore was a scene of turmoil, with people shrieking and tearing their hair as they looked out to sea.

"What has happened?" Pinocchio asked a little old woman.

"A poor old father lost his only son some time ago and today he built a tiny boat for himself in order to go in search of him across the ocean. The water is very stormy and we are afraid he will be drowned."

"Where is the boat?"

"There. Straight over there," answered the little old woman, pointing to a tiny shadow, no bigger than a nutshell, floating on the sea. Pinocchio looked hard and gave a sharp cry, "It's my father! It's my father!"

Meanwhile, the small boat, tossed about by the raging waters, appeared and disappeared into the waves. And Pinocchio, standing on a high rock, exhausted with searching, signaled by waving madly to him with his hand and cap and even his nose. It appeared as though Geppetto, far away from the shore, recognized his son, because he took off his cap and waved also. He seemed to be trying to make everyone understand that he would come back if he were able but, the sea was so rough that his oars were useless. Suddenly a huge wave swelled up and the boat vanished out of sight. They waited and waited for it, but it never appeared.

"Poor man!" said the fishermen and women on the shore, uttering their prayers as they turned to go home.

Just then a desperate cry was heard. Turning around, they saw Pinocchio dive into the sea and shout, "I'll save him! I'll save my father!"

The puppet, being made of wood, floated easily and swam like a fish in the rough water. Now and again he disappeared only to reappear once more. At last he was far away from land and completely lost to view.

"Poor boy!" cried the fishermen and women on the shore, and again they muttered a few prayers, as they returned home.

CHAPTER XXIV

Pinocchio reaches the Island of the Busy Bees and finds the Fairy
once more

Pinocchio, encouraged by the desire to find his father and to be there in time to save him, swam all night long. What a terrible storm there was! It pelted with rain and hail, and thunder crashed, lightning bolted, and altogether it was a wretched night.

At dawn, he saw, not far away from him, a long stretch of sand. It was an island in the middle of the sea. Pinocchio tried his best to get there, but he couldn't. The waves played with him and tossed him about as if he were a twig or a bit of straw. At last, and luckily for him, a tremendous wave tossed him to the very spot where he wanted to be. The blow from the wave was so strong that, as he fell to the ground, his joints crackled and almost snapped. But courageously, he jumped to his feet and cried, "Once more I have escaped with my life!"

Slowly the clouds lifted and the sun came out in its entire splendor and the sea became as calm and level as a lake. Then the puppet took his clothes and spread them on the sand to dry. He looked across the waters to see whether he might catch sight of a boat and a little man. He searched and he searched, but he saw nothing except sea and sky and far away a few sails, so small that they might have been birds.

"If only I knew the name of this island!" he longed to know. "If I even knew what kind of people I would find here, but whom should I ask? There is not anyone here."

The idea of being alone in so destitute a spot made him so upset that he was about to cry when he saw a big fish with his head above water, swimming nearby. Not knowing how to address him, the puppet said, "Ahoy there, Signor Fish, may I have a word with you?"

"Even two, if you want," said the fish, a very well-mannered Dolphin.

"Will you please tell me if, on this island, there are places where one may eat without necessarily being eaten?"

"Sure there are," answered the Dolphin. "In fact you'll find a spot nearby."

"And how do I get there?"

"Take that path on your left and follow your nose. You cannot miss it."

"Tell me another thing. You travel day and night through the sea. Did you perhaps meet a small boat with my father in it?"

"And who is you father?"

"He is the best father in the world, even as I am the worst son that can be had."

"In the storm last night," said the Dolphin, "the small boat must have capsized."

"And my father?"

"By now, he must have been swallowed by the Terrible Shark. The last few days, he has brought terror to these waters."

"Is this Shark very big?" asked Pinocchio, who was beginning to tremble with fright.

"Is he big?" replied the Dolphin. "Just to give you an idea of his size, let me say that he is bigger than a five story building and he has a mouth so wide and deep that an entire train and engine could easily get through it."

"*Mamma mia!*" exclaimed the terrified puppet, who quickly put on his clothes and turned to the dolphin to say, "Farewell, Signor Fish. Please excuse me, and thanks very much to you for your kindness." This said, he took the path at so swift a pace that he seemed to fly. Every small sound made him turn around in fear to see whether the Terrible Shark, five stories high and with a train in his mouth, was following him.

After walking for almost half an hour, he came to a small town called Busy Bee Town. The streets were filled with people rushing this way and that way about their business. Everyone worked, and everyone had something to do. Even if one were to search with a lantern, not one idle man or one tramp could be found.

"I can see," said Pinocchio at once wearily, "this is no place for me! I was not born for work." But in the meantime, he began to feel hungry, for it was twenty-four hours since he had eaten. What was to be done? There were only two means left to him in order to get something to eat. He either had to work or to beg.

He was ashamed to beg, because his father had always taught him that begging was only for the sick or the old. His father said that the real poor in this world, those unable to earn their bread with their own hands as a result of age or illness, were the only ones who deserved our help and compassion. All others should work, and if they didn't and felt hungry, so much the worse for them.

Just then a man passed by, looking worn out and dripping with sweat and working with great difficulty to pull two heavy carts loaded with coal. Pinocchio looked at him and thought him, judging by his appearance, to be a kind man. With eyes cast down in shame, Pinocchio asked, "Would you be so good as to give me a penny, for I am faint with hunger?"

"Not only one penny," answered the coal man. "I'll give you four if you will help me pull these two wagons."

"I am shocked!" answered the puppet, very much offended. "I would like you to know that I have neither been a donkey, nor have I ever pulled a wagon."

"So much the better for you!" said the coal man. "Then, my boy, if you are really faint with hunger, eat two slices of your pride, and I hope you don't get indigestion."

A few minutes after, a bricklayer passed by, carrying a pail filled with plaster on his shoulder.

"Good man, would you be kind enough to give a penny to a poor boy who is yawning from hunger?"

"Gladly," answered the bricklayer. "Come with me and help me to carry some plaster and, instead of one penny, I'll give you five."

"But the plaster is heavy," answered Pinocchio, "and the work is too hard for me."

"If the work is too hard for you, my boy, enjoy your yawns and may they bring you good luck!"

In less than a half an hour, at least twenty people passed and Pinocchio begged of each one to give him a penny, but they all answered, "Are you not ashamed? Instead of being a beggar in the streets, why don't you look for work and earn your own bread?"

Finally a little woman went by carrying two water jugs.

"Good woman, would you allow me to have a drink of water?" asked Pinocchio, who was burning up with thirst.

"With pleasure, my dear!" she answered, setting the two jugs on the ground.

After Pinocchio had his fill of water, he wiped his mouth and grumbled, "My thirst is gone. If I could only as easily get rid of my hunger!"

The good little woman listened to Pinocchio and immediately said, "If you help me to carry these jugs home, I'll give you a slice of bread." Pinocchio looked at the jug and said neither yes nor no. "And with the bread, I'll give you a nice dish of cauliflower with some white sauce on it." Pinocchio gave the jug another look and said neither yes nor no. "And after the cauliflower, some cake and jam."

Pinocchio could no longer resist her final bribe of cake and jam, and said firmly, "Very well. I'll take the jug home for you." The jug was very heavy and the puppet, not being strong enough to carry it with his hands, had to carry it balanced on his head.

When they arrived home, the little woman invited Pinocchio to sit at a small table and placed before him the bread, cauliflower, and cake. Pinocchio did not eat; he devoured. His stomach seemed like a bottomless pit.

His hunger finally satisfied, he raised his head to thank his kind benefactress. But he had not looked at her long when he stopped and sat there with his eyes opened wide and his mouth filled with bread and cauliflower, holding his fork in the air in surprise.

"What is all this surprise about?" asked the good woman, laughing.

"Because . . ." answered Pinocchio, stammering and stuttering, "because . . . you look like . . . you remind me of . . . yes, yes, the same voice, the same eyes, the same hair . . . yes, yes, yes, you also have the same blue hair she had . . . Oh, my little Fairy, my little Fairy! Tell me that it is you! Don't make me cry any longer! If you only knew! I have been miserable! I have suffered enough!"

And Pinocchio threw himself on the floor and clasped the knees of the mysterious little woman.

CHAPTER XXV

Pinocchio promises the Fairy to be good and to study, as he is growing tired of being a puppet, and wishes to become a real boy

If Pinocchio cried much longer, the little woman thought he would melt away, so she finally admitted that she was the little Fairy with Blue Hair. "You rascal of a puppet! How did you know it was me?" she asked, laughing.

"My love for you told me who you were."

"Do you remember? You left me when I was a young girl and now you find me a grown woman. I am much older. I could almost be your mother!"

"I am very glad of that, for now I can call you mother instead of sister. For a long time I have wanted a mother, just like other boys. But how did you grow so quickly?"

"That's a secret!"

"Tell it to me. I also want to grow a bit. Just look at me! I have never grown taller than knee height to a grasshopper."

"But you can't grow," answered the Fairy.

"Why not?"

"Because puppets never grow. They are born as puppets, they live as puppets, and they die as puppets."

"Oh, I'm tired of always being a puppet!" cried Pinocchio scornfully. "It's about time for me to grow into a man like everyone else."

"And you will if you learn to deserve it."

"Really? What can I do to deserve it?"

"It's a very simple matter. Try to act like a well-behaved child."

"Don't you think I do?"

"Far from it! Good boys are obedient, and you, on the contrary . . ."

"And I never obey."

"Good boys love study and work, but you . . ."

"And I, on the contrary, am a lazybones and a drifter all year round."

"Good boys always tell the truth."

"And I always tell lies."

"Good boys go to school."

"And I get a stomach ache when I go to school. From now on I'll be different."

"Do you promise?"

"I promise. I want to become a good boy and be a comfort to my father. Where is my poor father now?"

"I do not know."

"Will I ever be lucky enough to find him and embrace him once more?"

"I think so. I am absolutely sure of it."

Her answer made Pinocchio feel such elation that he grasped the Fairy's hands and kissed them wholeheartedly. Then lifting his face, he looked at her lovingly and asked, "Tell me, dearest Mother, it isn't true that you are dead, is it?"

"It doesn't seem so," answered the Fairy, smiling.

"If you only knew how much I suffered and how I cried when I read *'Here lies . . .'*"

"I know it, and for that I have forgiven you. The depth of your sorrow made me see that you have a kind heart. There is always hope for boys with hearts such as yours, though they may often be very mischievous. This is the reason why I have come so far to look for you. From now on, I'll be your own mother."

"Oh! How wonderful!" cried Pinocchio, jumping with joy.

"You will obey me always and do as I ask?"

"Gladly, very gladly, more than gladly!"

"Beginning tomorrow," said the Fairy, "you'll go to school every day."

Pinocchio's face fell a little downcast.

"Then you will choose the trade you like best."

Pinocchio turned more serious.

"What are you mumbling to yourself?" asked the Fairy.

"I was just saying," whined the puppet in a low voice, "that it seemed too late for me to go to school now."

"No, it is not. Remember it is never too late to learn."

"But I don't want a trade or a profession."

"Why?"

"Because work tires me out!"

"My dear boy," said the Fairy, "people who talk as you do usually end their days either in a prison or in a hospital. A man, remember, whether rich or poor, should do something in this world. No one can find happiness without work. A warning to the slacker! Slackness is a bad illness, and should be cured from early childhood. If not, by adulthood, recovery is almost impossible."

These words touched Pinocchio's heart. He lifted his eyes to his Fairy and said seriously, "I'll work, I'll study, I'll do all you tell me. After all, the life of a puppet has grown very tiresome to me and I want to become a boy, no matter how hard it is. You promise that, do you not?"

"Yes, I promise, and now it is up to you."

CHAPTER XXVI

Pinocchio goes to the seashore with his friends to see the Terrible Shark

In the morning, bright and early, Pinocchio started for school. Imagine what the boys said when they saw a puppet enter the classroom! They laughed until they cried. Everyone played tricks on him. One pulled his hat off, another tugged at his coat, and a third tried to paint a mustache under his nose. One even tried to tie strings to his hands and feet to make him dance.

For a while Pinocchio was very calm and quiet. Finally, however, he lost all patience and turning to his tormentors, he said to them sternly, "Careful, boys. I haven't come here to be ridiculed. I'll respect you and I ask for the same in return."

"Bravo, wise guy! You have spoken like a printed book!" howled the boys, bursting with laughter. One of the more impudent boys reached out to pull the puppet's nose. But he was not quick enough, for Pinocchio stretched his leg under the table and kicked him hard on the shin.

"Oh, what hard feet!" cried the boy, rubbing the spot where the puppet had kicked him.

"And what elbows! They are even harder than the feet!" shouted another, who had insulted him and received a punch in the stomach.

With a few well-targeted kicks and punches, Pinocchio acquired everyone's admiration. He gloried in his sudden popularity.

As the days passed into weeks, even the teacher began to praise him, because he was attentive, hard working, alert, and always the first to come in the morning, and the last to leave when school was over.

Pinocchio's only fault was that he had too many friends. Among these were many well-known rascals, who couldn't have cared less about their education or their futures.

The teacher warned him each day and the good Fairy also repeated to him many times, "Take care, Pinocchio! Those bad boys will sooner or later drive away your desire to study. Some day they will lead you into trouble."

"There's no such danger," answered the puppet, shrugging his shoulders and pointing to his forehead as if to say, "I'm smarter than you think I am."

So it happened that one day, as he was walking to school, he met some boys who ran up to him and said, "Have you heard the news?"

"No!"

"A Shark as big as a mountain has been seen near the seashore."

"Really? I wonder if it could be the same one I heard about when my father was drowned?"

"We are going to see it. Are you coming?"

"No, I can't. I must go to school."

"What do you care about school? You can go tomorrow. With a lesson more or less, we are always the same jackasses."

"And what will the teacher say?"

"Let him talk. That's what he's paid to do all day."

"And my mother?"

"Mothers don't know anything," answered those defiant boys.

"Do you know what I'll do?" said Pinocchio. "I have personal reasons, I want to see that Shark, too, but I'll go after school. I can see him then, just as well as now."

"What an idiot!" cried one of the boys. "Do you think that a fish of that size will hang around waiting for you? He comes and goes, and who knows when that might be?"

"How long does it take from here to the shore?" asked the puppet.

"One hour there and back."

"Then let's go. See who gets there first!" cried Pinocchio.

At the signal, the little gang, with their books in tow, dashed across the fields. Pinocchio led the way, running as if on wings, with the others following as fast as they could. Now and again, when he looked back and saw his followers, worn out and sweating in pursuit, he roared with laughter.

Unhappy puppet! If he had only known then the dreadful things that were to happen to him because of his disobedience!

CHAPTER XXVII

The great battle between Pinocchio and his schoolmates. One is wounded.
Pinocchio is arrested

Going like the wind, Pinocchio took a very short time to reach the seashore. He scanned the shoreline, but there was no sign of a Shark. The sea was as smooth as glass. He turned to his schoolmates and asked, "Hey there, guys! Where's that Shark?"

"He may have gone for breakfast," said one of them, grinning.

"Or, perhaps, he went to bed for a little nap," scoffed another.

From their answers and the smirking that proceeded, Pinocchio understood the boys had played a trick on him. "What now?" he said angrily to them. "What's the joke?"

"Guess what? The joke is on you!" cried his tormentors, splitting their sides with laughter.

"What's the joke?"

"That we have made you skip out of school to be with us. Aren't you embarrassed about being such an honor student and spending too much time on your schoolwork that you don't know how to have fun?"

"And what is it to you, if I do study?"

"What does the teacher think of us, you mean?"

"Why?"

"Don't you see? If you study and we don't, you make us look bad. After all, it's only fair to look out for ourselves."

"What do you want me to do?"

"You should hate school and books and teachers, just like we do. They are your worst enemies, and they like to keep you feeling miserable."

"And if I keep studying, what will you do to me?"

"You'll have us to pay back!"

"Really, you make me smile," answered the puppet, shaking his head.

"Hey, Pinocchio," called out the tallest boy, "that will do! We are sick of listening to you bragging about yourself, you show-off! You might not be afraid of us, but remember we are not afraid of you, either! You are alone, aren't you, and there are seven of us."

"Like the seven deadly sins," said Pinocchio, tauntingly.

"Did you hear that? He has insulted us. He called us the seven deadly sins."

"Pinocchio, apologize for that, or watch out!"

"Cuckoo!" said the puppet, thumbing his nose at them.

"You'll be sorry!"

"Cuckoo!"

"We'll beat you up badly!"

"Cuckoo!"

"You'll go home with a busted nose!"

"Cuckoo!"

"Alright, in that case! Take that, and keep it for your supper!" shouted a bully, who slammed his fist into Pinocchio's head.

Pinocchio responded with a strike and that signaled the beginning of the fight. In a few moments, it raged hot and heavy on both sides. Pinocchio, though alone, defended himself bravely. With his wooden feet, he delivered swift kicks to his opponents and kept them at bay. Wherever a blow landed, it left a throbbing pain. All the boys could do was to tear away from Pinocchio, reeling in all directions.

Enraged at not being able to outmaneuver the puppet at close range, they started to hurl all kinds of books at him. Anthologies, geographies, histories, and grammars flew in all directions. But Pinocchio had a keen eye and was fast on his feet, and the books only flew over his head, landed in the sea, and floated away.

The fish, thinking they might be good to eat, swam to the surface of the water in great numbers. Some took a nibble, some took a bite, but no sooner had they tasted a page or two, than they spat them out and made wry faces, as if to say, "What a horrible flavor! Our own stuff is so much better!"

Meanwhile, the fighting got worse. The screaming and shouting disturbed a large crab that crawled slowly out of the water and called out hoarsely with a voice that sounded like a trombone suffering from a sore throat, "Stop fighting, you brutes! These clashes rarely end well. These battles are bound to lead to more trouble!"

Poor crab! He might as well have spoken to the wind. Instead of listening to his good advice, Pinocchio turned to him and said as roughly as he knew how, "Shut up, crab face! It would be better for you to suck a few cough drops to get rid of your rough throat. Get back to bed and sleep! You will feel better in the morning."

In the meantime, the boys, having used all their books for ammunition, looked around for more. Seeing Pinocchio's bundle lying idle nearby, they managed to get hold of it. One of the books was a very large arithmetic textbook, heavily bound in leather. It was Pinocchio's favorite. Among all his books, he liked that one the best. Thinking it would make a terrific missile, one of the boys grabbed it and threw it with all his strength at Pinocchio's head. But instead of hitting the puppet, the book struck one of the other boys who fell senseless to the ground, after he cried out faintly, "Oh, help me, please! I am dying!"

The sight of that pale, deathly victim frightened the boys so much that they all turned and ran away, except Pinocchio. Although scared by the horror of what had happened, he ran and soaked his handkerchief in the sea and bathed his unfortunate schoolmate's head. He deplored loudly, "Eugene! My poor Eugene! Open your eyes and look at me! Why don't you answer? I was not the one who hit you, you know. Believe me, I didn't do it. Open your eyes, Eugene. If you keep them shut, I'll die, too. Oh, dear me, how will I ever go home now? How will I ever look at my little mother again? What will happen to me? Where should I go? Where should I hide? Oh, it would have been a thousand times better, if only I had gone to school! Why did I listen to those boys? They were always a bad influence! To think that the teacher had warned my mother, and me, too! 'Beware of bad company!' That's what she said, but I'm stupid and obstinate. I listen, but I always do as I want. Then I pay for my mistakes. I've never had a moment's peace since I've been born! Oh, dear! What will become of me? What will become of me?"

Pinocchio continued to cry and moan and beat his head and call out his friend's name over and over. Suddenly he heard heavy steps approaching. He looked up and saw two tall carabinieri near him.

"What are you doing stretched out on the ground?" they asked Pinocchio.

"I'm helping this schoolmate of mine."

"Is he sick?"

"I should say so," said one of the carabinieri, bending to look at Eugene. "This boy has been wounded on the temple. Who has hit him?"

"Not I," stammered the puppet, breathlessly.

"If it wasn't you, who was it, then?"

"Not I," repeated Pinocchio.

"What was used to strike him?"

"This book," said Pinocchio, and he picked up the arithmetic textbook to show it to the officer.

"And whose book is this?"

"Mine."

"Enough!" he said.

"Not another word!" said the other. "Get up and come along with us."

"But I . . . ."

"Come with us!"

"But I am innocent."

"Come with us!"

Before starting out, the officers called out to several fishermen passing by in a boat and said to them, "Take care of this young boy who has been hurt. Take him home and bandage his head. Tomorrow we'll come for him." They then took hold of Pinocchio and, crushing him between them, said in a rough voice, "March! And quickly, or it will be even worse for you!"

They did not have to repeat their orders. The puppet walked swiftly along the road to the village, but he had no idea what was happening to him. He thought he was having a nightmare. He felt sick. Everything appeared in a haze. His legs trembled, his mouth went dry, and he couldn't stammer a single word even if he tried. Yet, in spite of feeling petrified, he agonized at the thought of passing by his good little Fairy's house. What would she say if she saw him marching between two carabinieri?

When they had just reached the village, a sudden gust of wind blew away Pinocchio's cap and it flew down the street. "Would you allow me," the puppet asked the carabinieri, "to run after my cap?"

"Very well. Go, and hurry."

The puppet dashed toward his cap and picked it up but instead of putting it back on, he stuck it between his teeth and raced toward the sea. He shot away like a bullet out of a gun. The carabinieri, judging that it would be impossible to catch him, set a large mastiff after him, one that had won first prize in all the dog races. Pinocchio ran fast and the dog ran faster.

The noise and commotion sent people running to their windows or crowding in the street, curious to see who would win the contest. But they were disappointed, because Pinocchio and the dog raised so much dust on the road that after a few moments it was impossible to see them.

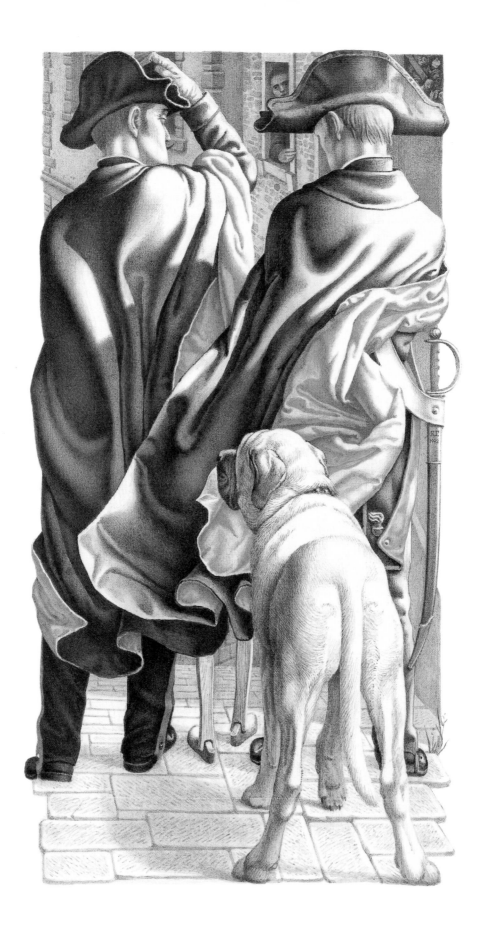

CHAPTER XXVIII

Pinocchio runs the danger of being fried in a pan like a fish

During the wild chase, there was a terrible moment when the puppet thought he almost lost the race and Alidoro (since this was the name of the mastiff) ran so close that he almost caught Pinocchio. The puppet heard the beast huffing and puffing loudly and sometimes he even felt his hot breath close behind him. Luckily, by this time, he was close to the shore, and the sea was just a short distance away.

Just as he set foot on the beach, Pinocchio gave a leap and plunged into the sea. Alidoro tried to stop but he was running so fast that he couldn't, and landed far out in the water. Strange though it may seem, the dog could not swim. He beat the water with his paws to hold himself up, but the harder he tried, the deeper he sank. As he stuck his head out once more, the poor animal was panic stricken, and he barked, "I am drowning! I am drowning!"

"Drown!" answered Pinocchio from far away, happy to have escaped.

"Help, Pinocchio, dear little Pinocchio! Save me from drowning!"

The puppet, having a very kind heart after all, was moved to compassion by Alidoro's cries of suffering. He turned toward the poor animal and said to him, "But if I help you, will you promise not to bother me again by running after me?"

"I promise! I promise! Only hurry, for if you wait another second, I'll be dead and gone!"

Pinocchio paused a moment and considered that his father had often told him that a kind deed is never lost, then he swam to Alidoro and caught hold of his tail to drag him to the shore.

The poor dog was so weak he could not stand. He had swallowed so much salt water that he was swollen like a balloon. However, Pinocchio, not wishing to trust him too much, threw himself into the sea again. As he swam away, he called out, "Goodbye, Alidoro, good luck and remember me to the family!"

"Goodbye, little Pinocchio," answered the dog. "A thousand thanks for having saved me from death. You did me a good turn, and, in this world, what is given is always returned. If the chance comes, I will be there."

Pinocchio went on swimming close to shore. At last, he thought he had reached a safe place. Glancing up and down the beach, he noticed a cave in the rocks, with a spiral of smoke drifting out of its opening. "There must be a fire in that cave, and that's good" he thought. "I'll dry my clothes and warm myself, and then I'll see what comes next" he decided.

Having made up his mind, Pinocchio swam to the rocks but as he started to climb, he felt something underneath lifting him up higher and higher. He tried to escape, but it was too late. To his great amazement, he discovered that he was caught inside a huge net, in a mass of fish of all sizes and varieties, which were fighting and struggling desperately get free.

He saw a fisherman come out of the cave, so ugly and hideous looking that Pinocchio thought he was a sea monster. To describe him, his head was covered with a thick green patch of weeds instead of hair, and green was the color of his skin, his eyes, and the long beard that hung to the ground. When he stood up, he looked like a giant green lizard with arms and legs.

When the fisherman pulled the net out of the sea, he cried out excitedly, "What a lucky day for me! Once more I'll have a fine fish dinner!"

"Thank goodness I'm not a fish!" said Pinocchio, trying to bolster his courage.

The fisherman took the net full of fish to the cave. It was a dark, smoky, gloomy place. In the middle of it, a pan full of oil sizzled over a smoky fire, sending out a repugnant smell of grease.

"Now, let's see what kind of fish we have caught today!" said the Green Fisherman. He put a huge hand into the net and pulled out a handful of mullets. "Choice mullets, these!" he said, after looking at them and sniffing them with pleasure. After that, he threw them into a large, empty tub. He repeated this performance many times. As he pulled each fish out of the net, his mouth watered with the thought of the good dinner coming, and he said:

"Choice fish, these bass!"

"Very tasty, these whitefish!"

"Delicious flounders, these!"

"What beautiful crabs!"

"And these dear little anchovies are excellent!"

As you can well imagine, the bass, the flounders, the whitefish, and even the little anchovies all went together into the tub to keep the mullets company.

The last to come out of the net was Pinocchio. As soon as the fisherman pulled him out, his green eyes opened wide with surprise, and he cried out cautiously, "What kind of fish is this? I don't remember ever eating anything like it." He looked at him closely and after turning him over and over, he said at last, "I guess he must be a crab!"

Pinocchio, humiliated at being mistaken for a crab, said resentfully, "What nonsense!

A crab indeed! I am no such thing. Careful how you deal with me! I am a puppet, I want you to know."

"A puppet?" asked the fisherman. "I must admit that a puppet fish is an entirely new kind of thing to me. I'll enjoy eating you even better."

"Eating me? But can't you understand that I'm not a fish? Aren't you listening? I can speak and think as you do?"

"It's true," answered the fisherman, "but since I see that you are a fish, well able to talk and think as I do, I'll treat you with all due respect."

"And that is . . .?"

"That is, as a sign of my regard and high esteem, I'll leave you to choose how you are to be cooked. Do you wish to be fried in a pan, or do you prefer to be cooked with a tomato sauce?"

"To tell you the truth," answered Pinocchio, "if I must choose, I would much rather go free so I may return home!"

"Are you joking? Do you think I would lose the opportunity to taste such a rare fish? A puppet fish does not come very often to these seas. Leave it to me. I'll fry you in the pan with the others. I know you'll like it. It's always a comfort to find oneself in good

company."

The unlucky puppet, hearing this, began to cry and wail and beg. With tears stream-ing down his cheeks, he said, "How much better if I had gone to school! I should not have listened to my schoolmates and now I am paying for it! Oh! Oh! Oh!"

As he struggled and squirmed like an eel to escape from him, the Green Fisherman took a strong cord and tied him like a piece of salami, and threw him into the bottom of the tub with the others. Then he pulled a wooden bowl full of flour out of a cupboard and started to roll the fish into it, one by one. When they were covered with flour, he threw them into the pan.

The first to dance in the hot oil were the mullets followed by the bass, then the whitefish, the flounders, and the anchovies. Pinocchio's turn came last. The end seemed inevitable and he began to tremble with so much fright that he was speechless. All he could do was to stare wide-eyed with a look that begged the Green Fisherman to spare him.

The Green Fisherman paid no attention to Pinocchio and flipped him several times until he was completely dredged in flour. Then he took him by the head and . . .

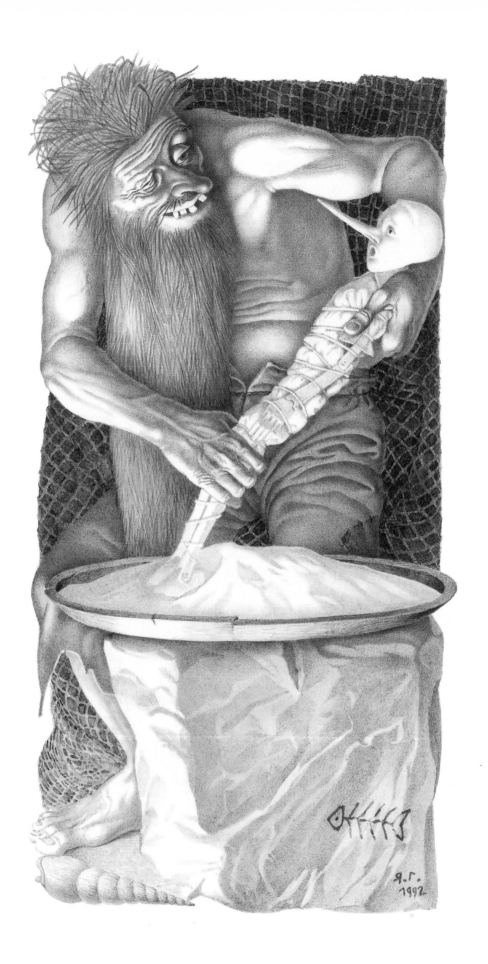

CHAPTER XXIX

Pinocchio returns to the Fairy's house and she promises him that the next day he will no longer be a puppet and will become a boy. A wonderful breakfast party of caffè-e-latte *to celebrate the great event*

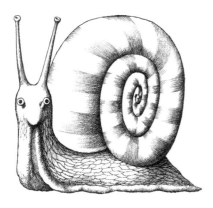

Concerned with what the fisherman had said, Pinocchio knew he had lost all hope of being saved. He closed his eyes tightly and braced himself for the final moment. Suddenly, a large dog, attracted by the smell of the boiling oil, came running into the cave. "Get out!" cried the fisherman threateningly, holding onto the helpless puppet.

The poor dog was very hungry, and he kept whining and wagging his tail, as if to say, "Give me a bite of the fish and I'll be out of your way."

"Get out, I say!" repeated the fisherman.

He stepped back to give the dog a kick, but the dog was exceedingly hungry and refused to budge. He turned in a rage toward the fisherman and growled, baring his terrible fangs. And at that moment, a pathetic little voice said, "Save me, Alidoro, if you don't, I'll be fried!"

The dog immediately recognized Pinocchio's voice. He was astonished that the voice came from the little flour-covered bundle held in the fisherman's hand. Then what did he do? With one great leap, he snatched the bundle in his mouth, holding it lightly between his teeth, ran through the door, and disappeared like a flash of lightening! The fisherman, furious about seeing his meal stolen from under his nose, ran after the dog, but a bad fit of coughing made him stop and turn back.

Meanwhile, as soon as Alidoro found the road that led to the village, he stopped and gently lowered Pinocchio to the ground. "How can I thank you!" said the puppet.

"It is not necessary," answered the dog. "You saved me once, and what is given is always returned. Are we not in this world to help each another?"

"But how did you get in that cave?"

"I was lying here on the sand more dead than alive, when I noticed a delicious smell of fried fish. It tickled my hunger and I followed it. Imagine if I had come a moment later!"

"Don't speak about it," wailed Pinocchio, still trembling with fright. "Don't say a word. If you had come a moment later, I would be fried, eaten, and digested by this time. *Brrrr!* I just shiver at the thought of it."

Alidoro laughingly held out his paw to the puppet, who gave him a warm hand-shake, feeling certain that he and the dog had become good friends. Then they waved each other goodbye and the dog went away home.

Pinocchio, left alone, walked toward a little hut nearby, where an old man was seated in the sunshine and asked, "Tell me, good man, have you heard any news of a poor boy with a wounded head, whose name was Eugene?"

"The boy was brought to this hut and now . . ."

"Now he is dead?" interrupted Pinocchio, filled with sorrow.

"Oh no. He is quite alive and has already returned home."

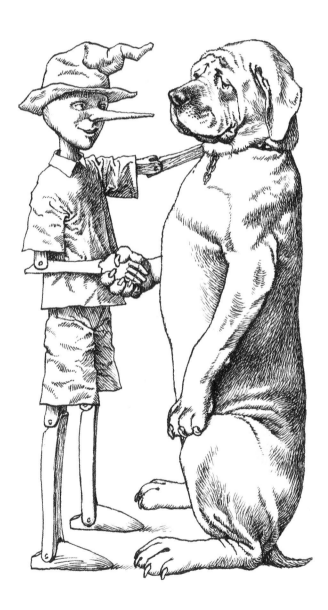

"Really? Really?" cried the puppet, jumping with joy. "Then the wound was not serious?"

"It might have been serious, or even fatal." answered the old man and continued, "That was a heavy book thrown at his head."

"And who threw it?"

"A schoolmate of his, a certain Pinocchio."

"And who is this Pinocchio?" asked the puppet, pretending to be unaware.

"They say he is a nothing but a troublemaker, a runaway, a crazy devil."

"Lies! All lies!"

"Do you know this Pinocchio?"

"Only by sight!" answered the puppet.

"And what do you think of him?" asked the old man.

"I think he's a very nice boy, who likes to study, and is well-behaved and respectful to his father and family."

While he was telling these huge lies about himself, Pinocchio touched his nose and discovered it had grown twice as long as it was. Afraid, he cried out, "Don't listen to me, good man! All the wonderful things I have said are not true at all. I know Pinocchio well and he is truly wicked, lazy and misbehaved. Instead of going to school, he runs away with his schoolmates to have a good time." After he spoke, his nose returned to its natural size.

"Why are you so white-faced?" the old man asked suddenly.

"I will tell you. Without realizing it, I rubbed myself against a freshly white-washed wall," he lied, ashamed to say that he had been prepared for a frying pan.

"What have you done with your coat and your hat and your trousers?"

"I met some thieves and they robbed me bare. Tell me, my good man, have you any spare clothes to lend me, so I can go home dressed?"

"My boy, as for clothes, I only have a sack I use to keep hops. If you want it, take it. There it is."

Pinocchio did not think twice about accepting the empty sack. He cut a big hole at the top and two at the sides and slipped it over his head like a shirt. Although he was barely dressed, he started out toward the village.

Along the way, he felt very uneasy. In fact, he felt so unsure that he went along taking two steps forward and one step back. On his way, he thought, "How will I ever face my good little Fairy? What will she say when she sees me? Will she forgive this last trick of mine? I am sure she won't. Oh, no, she won't. I deserve it, as usual, because I am a cheater and never keep my promises!"

Pinocchio came to the village late at night. It was very dark and raining so heavily that he could not see a thing. He went directly to the Fairy's house, firmly resolved to knock at the door. When he got there, he lost courage and ran back a few steps. A second time he went to the door and ran back again. A third time he did the same. The fourth time, before he had time to lose his courage, he grasped the knocker and gave

it a faint rap.

He waited and waited and waited. Finally, after a full half an hour, a window opened on the top floor of the four-storied house and a large Snail looked out. A tiny light glowed on top of her head. "Who knocks at this late hour?" she called.

"Is the Fairy home?" asked the puppet.

"The Fairy is asleep and does not wish to be disturbed. Who are you?"

"It's me."

"Who's that?"

"Pinocchio."

"Who is Pinocchio?"

"The puppet, the one who lives in the Fairy's house."

"Oh, I understand," said the Snail. "Wait for me there. I'll come down to open the door for you."

"Hurry, please! I am dying of cold."

"My boy, I am a snail and snails are never in a hurry."

An hour passed, two hours, and the door was still closed. Pinocchio, who was trembling with fear and shivering from cold rain on his back, knocked a second time, this time louder than before. At the second knock, a window on the third floor opened and the Snail looked out.

"Dear little Snail," cried Pinocchio from the street. "I have been waiting two hours for you! Two hours on a dreadful night like this are as long as two years. Hurry, please!"

"My boy," answered the Snail in a calm voice, "my dear boy, I am a snail and snails are never in a hurry." Then the window closed.

A few minutes later midnight struck, and then one o'clock, and then two o'clock, yet the door remained closed! Then Pinocchio, losing his patience, grabbed the knocker with both hands, determined to make a noise loud enough to startle the household. As soon as he touched the knocker, however, it turned into a squirming eel and slithered into the darkness.

"Really?" cried Pinocchio, who was blinded by rage. "If the knocker is gone, I can still use my feet." He stepped back and gave the door a most strong, solid kick. In fact, he kicked so hard that his foot went straight through the door and took his leg almost to the knee. No matter how he pulled and tugged, he could not pull it out. There he remained, as if nailed to the door. Poor Pinocchio! For the rest of the night, he was stuck with one foot through the door.

As dawn was breaking, the door finally opened. That indefatigable Snail had taken exactly nine hours to go from the fourth floor to the street. How she must have raced!

"What are you doing with your foot through the door?" she asked the puppet, laughing.

"It was an accident. Pretty little Snail, won't you try to free me from this terrible situation?"

106

"My boy, we need a carpenter here and I have never been one."

"Ask the Fairy to help me!"

"The Fairy is asleep and does not want to be disturbed."

"But what do you want me to do, with my leg stuck in the door like this?"

"Enjoy yourself by counting the ants which pass by."

"Bring me something to eat, at least, for I am faint with hunger."

"At once!"

Three and half-hours later, Pinocchio watched her return with a silver tray on her head. On it, there was bread, roast chicken, and fruit. "Here is the breakfast the Fairy sends to you," said the Snail. The sight of all these good things made the puppet feel much better. How disillusioned he felt when he tasted the food and discovered that the bread was made of chalk, the chicken of cardboard, and the fruit of painted alabaster! He wanted to cry or give up in despair. He wanted to throw away the tray and everything on it. Instead, either from disgust or weakness, he fainted to the floor.

When he was revived, he was lying on a sofa and the Fairy was seated near him. "This time also I forgive you," said the Fairy to him. "But be careful not to get into mischief again."

Pinocchio promised to study and to behave himself, and he kept his word for the remainder of the year. At the end of it, he passed first in all his examinations, and he got such an excellent report that the Fairy said to him happily, "Tomorrow your wish will come true."

"And what is it?"

"Tomorrow you will cease to be a puppet and will become a real boy."

Pinocchio was happy as ever! All his friends and schoolmates must be invited to celebrate the great event. The Fairy promised to prepare two hundred cups of *caffè-e-latte* and four hundred puffed rolls buttered inside and out. The day promised to be a lot of fun, but . . .

Unfortunately in a puppet's life there is always a *but* which threatens to spoil everything.

CHAPTER XXX

Pinocchio, instead of becoming a boy, runs away to Play Land with his friend, Lampwick

Pinocchio naturally asked the Fairy for permission to give out the invitations to the party. "Indeed, you may invite all your friends. Only remember to return home before dark. Do you understand?"

"I promise to be back in one hour," replied the puppet.

"Take care, Pinocchio! Boys give promises very easily, but they as easily forget them."

"But I am not like those others. When I give my word I keep it."

"We will see. If you disobey, you will be the one to suffer and no one else."

"Why?"

"Because boys who do not listen to those with experience always end up in trouble."

"I'm proof of that," said Pinocchio, "but from now on, I'll obey."

"We will see if you are telling the truth." Without adding another word, the puppet said goodbye to the good Fairy and, singing and dancing, he left the house.

In a little more than an hour, he had invited all his friends to the party. Some gladly accepted immediately, but others had to be coaxed. When they heard that the puffed rolls were to be buttered inside and out, they all accepted the invitation by saying, "We'll come just to please you."

Now everyone knew that, among Pinocchio's friends, there was one he liked best of all. The boy's real name was Romeo, but everyone called him Lampwick, because he was tall and thin and had a downcast look about him. Lampwick was the laziest boy in the school and the biggest troublemaker, but Pinocchio liked him the most.

That day, Pinocchio went straight to his friend's house to invite him to the party, but Lampwick was not at home. He went a second time, and again a third, but still without success. Where could he be? Pinocchio searched here and there and everywhere, and finally found him hiding under the porch of a farmhouse.

"What are you doing there?" asked Pinocchio, running up to him.

"I am waiting to leave at midnight."

"Where are you going?"

"Far, far, far away!"

"And I have gone to your house three times to look for you!"

"What did you want me for?"

"Haven't you heard the news? Don't you know what good luck is mine?"

"What is it?"

"Tomorrow I end my days as a puppet and become a boy, like you and all my other friends."

"Well, good for you!" said Lampwick, sarcastically.

"Will I see you at my party tomorrow?"

"But I've told you that I am leaving tonight."

"At what time?"

"At midnight."

"And where are you going?"

"To the best country in the whole world! A wonderful place with everything and anything you'd ever want!"

"What is it called?"

"It is called Play Land. Why don't you come, too?"

"Me? Oh, no!"

"You are making a big mistake, Pinocchio. Believe me, if you don't come, you'll regret it. Where else can you find a place to suit you and me better? No schools, no teachers, no books! In a place like that, there is no such thing as study. Here, it is only Saturday that we have no school. In Play Land, every day is a Saturday, except for Sunday. Vacation begins on the first day of January and ends on the last day of December. That is the spot for me! All countries should be like it! How happy we would all be!"

"But how does one spend the day in Play Land?"

"Days are spent having a ball of fun from morning until night. At night one goes to bed, and next morning, the good times begin all over again. What do you think of it?"

"Hmm . . .!" said Pinocchio, nodding his head, and thinking, "Wouldn't it agree with me perfectly?"

"Do you want to go with me? Yes, or no? You have to make up your mind."

"No, no, no, and again no! I have promised my kind Fairy to become a good boy, and I intend to keep my word. There, you see, the sun is setting. I must leave you and run. Goodbye and have a great trip!"

"Where are you going in such a hurry?"

"Home. My good Fairy wants me to return home before night."

"Stay two more minutes."

"It's already late!"

"Only two minutes."

"And if the Fairy gives me a scolding?"

"Let her scold. She'll stop when she gets tired," said Lampwick.

"Are you going alone or with others?"

"Alone? There will be more than a hundred of us!"

"Will you be walking?"

"A wagon will be here at midnight to take me and the rest to the border of that excellent land."

"How I wish midnight would strike!"

"Why?"

"To see you all leave together."

"Stay here a little longer and you will see us!"

"No, no. I want to return home."

"Stay two more minutes."

"I have stayed too long as it is. The Fairy will be worried."

"Poor Fairy! Is she afraid the bats will eat you?"

"Listen, Lampwick," said the puppet, "are you really sure there are no schools in Play Land?"

"Not a trace."

"Not even one teacher?"

"Not one."

"And one does not have to study?"

"Never, never, never."

"What an amazing country!" said Pinocchio, with longing. "What a beautiful land! I have never been there, but I can just imagine it."

"Why don't you come, too?"

"It is useless for you to tempt me! I told you I promised my good Fairy to behave myself, and I am going to keep my word."

"Goodbye, then, and remember me to the grammar schools and the high schools if you should meet them on the way."

"Goodbye, Lampwick. Have a good trip. Enjoy yourself, and remember your friends once in a while."

Having wished Lampwick farewell, the puppet started on his way home. Then he stopped, and turned around to his friend, and asked, "Are you sure, in that country, six Saturdays and one Sunday make each week?"

"Absolutely sure!"

"And that vacation begins on the first day of January and ends on the last day of December?"

"Absolutely positively sure!"

"What an amazing country!" repeated Pinocchio, uncertain about what to do. Then, with a fixed determination, he said hurriedly, "Goodbye for the last time, and safe travels!"

"Goodbye."

"How soon will you go?"

"Within two hours."

"It's too bad! If it were only an hour, I might wait with you."

"And the Fairy?"

"By this time I'm late, and one hour more or less doesn't make much difference."

"Poor Pinocchio! And if the Fairy gives you a scolding?"

"Let her scold. She'll stop when she gets tired," said Pinocchio.

Meanwhile, the night had become darker and darker. All at once, they saw a small light glimmering in the distance and heard the sound of bells tinkling, and the trill, faint noise of a trumpet like the disquieting buzz of mosquitoes. "There it is!" cried Lampwick, jumping to his feet.

"What?" whispered Pinocchio.

"The wagon is coming to get me. For the last time, are you coming or not?"

"Tell me again, is it really true in that country, boys never have to study?"

"Never, never, never!"

"What a wonderful, excellent, amazing country!"

CHAPTER XXXI

After five months of play, Pinocchio wakes up one fine morning and finds a great surprise waiting him

Finally the wagon appeared. It arrived without a sound, because its wheels were padded with straw and rags. Twelve pairs of donkeys, all of the same size, and each one of a different color drew the wagon. Some were gray and others white, and others a mixture of brown and black. Scattered among them were a few with vibrant yellow and blue stripes. The strangest thing of all was that those twenty-four donkeys were not shod in iron, like other beasts of burden, but wore laced leather boots just like the ones boys wear.

And the driver of the wagon?

Imagine a fat, little man, wider than his height, as round and shiny as a ball of butter, with a rosy face like an apple, a fawning smile on his little mouth, and a voice that purred like a cat. No sooner did any boy see him than he was charmed and longing to be taken in the wagon to that wonderful place called Play Land.

In fact, the wagon was so tightly packed with boys between the ages of eight and twelve that it looked like a tin of sardines. They were very uncomfortable, piled one on top of the other, and could hardly breathe. Yet, nobody complained. The happy anticipation of knowing that in a few hours they would reach a country where there were no schools, no books, and no teachers gave the boys no reason to feel hungry, thirsty, sleepy, or uncomfortable.

No sooner had the wagon stopped than the little man turned to Lampwick and asked, bowing and grinning, "Tell me, my dear boy, do you want to come to my wonderful land?"

"You bet I do!"

"But I warn you, my little dear, the wagon is quite full and there's no more room."

"Never mind," answered Lampwick. "If there's no room inside, I can sit on the top of the coach," and with one leap, he climbed on top.

"And what about you, my darling?" asked the little man, turning politely to Pinocchio. "What are you going to do? Will you come with us, or will you stay?"

"I'll stay here," answered Pinocchio. "I want to return home. I prefer my studies and plan to succeed in life."

"All the best to your plans, then!"

"Pinocchio!" Lampwick called out. "Listen to me. Come with us and we'll have a great time together!"

"No, thank you anyway."

"Come with us and we'll all have a great time!" yelled four other voices from the wagon.

"Come with us and all of us will always have a great time!" shouted all one hundred and more boys in the wagon.

"And if I go with you, what will my good Fairy say?" asked the puppet, whose good intentions were beginning to weaken.

"Don't worry so much. Only think that we are going to a land where we will be allowed to make the biggest racket we like from morning until night."

Pinocchio did not answer but clamped his lips together and sighed deeply once, twice, and a third time. Finally he abandoned all resolve and said, "Make room for me. I want to go, too!"

"The seats are all taken," answered the little man, "but to show you how much I care, you may take my place as coachman."

"What about you?"

"I'll walk."

"No, you shouldn't do that. I could not permit such a thing. I much prefer riding one of these donkeys," cried Pinocchio.

No sooner said than done. He approached the first donkey and tried to mount it. Suddenly the little animal bolted and gave Pinocchio such a terrible kick in the stomach that he was thrown to the ground with his legs in the air. The whole company of runaways instantly burst into laughter. The little man just smiled. He went up to the rebellious animal, and, still smiling, leaned toward him tenderly and bit off half his right ear.

In the meantime, Pinocchio got up and leaped onto the donkey's back. The leap was done so perfectly that all the boys shouted, "Bravo for Pinocchio!" and clapped their hands in applause. The donkey gave an abrupt kick with his two hind feet, sending Pinocchio sprawling in the middle of the road again. The boys shouted with laughter again. Yet, the little man just smiled and leaned toward the animal and, pretending to kiss him, he bit off half his left ear.

"You can get on him now, my boy," he said to Pinocchio. "Have no fear. That donkey was bothered about something, but I have spoken to him and now he seems quiet and reasonable."

Pinocchio climbed on the donkey's back and the wagon started on its way. While the donkeys galloped along the stony road, the puppet imagined he heard a very low voice whispering to him, "Poor numbskull! You have done as you wished. But you are going to be sorry before very long."

Pinocchio, greatly frightened, looked about him to see where the words had originated, but he saw no one. The donkeys galloped, the wagon rolled on smoothly, the boys slept, Lampwick snored like a dormouse and the little man sat at the reins, whistling softly to himself.

After a mile or so, Pinocchio again heard the same faint voice whispering, "Listen, you wooden spoon! Boys who stop studying and turn their backs upon books and schools and teachers in order to give all their time to nonsense and games will sooner or later come to hard times. How well I know this! How well I can prove it to you! A day will come when you will cry bitterly like I am, but it will be too late!"

These whispers made the puppet grow even more frightened. He jumped to the ground, ran up to the donkey, cupped his head, and looked at him seriously. Pinocchio was taken by surprise to see that the donkey was crying . . . crying just like a boy! "Hey, signor little man!" called Pinocchio to the wagon driver. "Something strange thing is going on here! This donkey is crying."

"Let him cry. When he gets married, he will have time to laugh," he chuckled.

"Have you perhaps taught him to speak?"

"No, he only learned to mumble a few words when he lived for three years with a band of performing dogs."

"Poor beast!"

"Come, come," said the little man, "do not lose time over a sniveling donkey. Get back quickly and let us go. The night is cool and the road is long." Pinocchio obeyed without another word. The wagon started again. Toward dawn the next morning, they finally reached Play Land.

This great land was entirely different from any other place in the world. Its population was entirely comprised of boys. The oldest were about fourteen years of age and the youngest eight. In the street, there was such a racket of noise and shouting and trumpet blowing that it was deafening. Everywhere groups of boys were gathered together. Some played at marbles, at hopscotch, at ball. Others rode on bicycles or on wooden horses. Some played at blindman's-buff, others at tag. Here a group played circus clowns and there another sang and danced. A few turned somersaults, while others walked on their hands with their feet in the air. Generals passed by wearing paper uniforms, leading regiments of cardboard soldiers. Laughter, shrieking, howling, whooping, yelling, and clapping followed this parade. One boy cackled like a chicken, another crowed like a rooster, and a third roared like a lion. All together, it was such a pandemonium that it was necessary to put cotton in one's ears.

The squares were filled with small wooden theaters, overflowing with boys from morning until night, and on the walls of the houses, written in chalk, were mispelled sayings like "Hurra for PleyLand!" and "Down wit Skools!" and "No more Rithmetik!" and "Fun Forefer."

As soon as they set foot there, Pinocchio, Lampwick, and all the boys who had

traveled with them started out on an investigative tour. They wandered everywhere and peeked into every nook and corner, house and theater. Soon they became everybody's friends. Who could be happier? What with entertainment and parties, the hours, the days, and the weeks passed like lightning. "Oh, what a beautiful life this is!" said Pinocchio each time he chanced to meet his friend Lampwick.

"Was I right or was I wrong?" asked Lampwick. "And to think you did not want to come! To think that you had the grand idea to return home to your Fairy and to waste time studying! If you are free from pencils and books and school these days, you owe it to my sound advice. Don't you admit it? After all, only true friends count."

"It's the truth, Lampwick, it's the truth. If I am really a happy boy today, it is all because of you. Just think that the teacher used to say, 'Do not go with that Lampwick! He is a bad companion and some day he will lead you astray.'"

"Poor teacher!" said the other, nodding his head. "I know, he thought I was a wretch and liked to say bad things about me. But I'm not going to hold a grudge against him."

"You're the best!" said Pinocchio, warmly embracing his friend.

Five months passed by, and the boys continued playing and enjoying themselves from morning until night, without ever seeing a book, or a desk, or a school. But, my dear readers, there came a morning when Pinocchio awoke and found a great surprise awaiting him, a surprise which made him feel very unhappy, as you will see.

CHAPTER XXXII

Pinocchio gets donkey ears. In a little while he changes into a real donkey and begins to bray

What was Pinocchio's surprise?

I will tell you, my dear readers. On awakening, Pinocchio put his hand up to his head and there he discovered . . . guess! He discovered that, during the night, his ears had grown at least ten full inches!

Remember that the puppet, even from his birth, had very small ears, so small that they could hardly be seen to the naked eye. Imagine how he felt when he noticed that overnight those two tiny ears had become as long as shoe brushes!

He went in search of a mirror, but not finding any, he simply filled a basin with water and looked at his reflection. There he saw what he never would have wished to see. A beautiful pair of donkey's ears protruded from his silhouette.

I leave you to think of the awful grief, shame, and despair he felt. He began to cry and to scream, and knocked his head against the wall, but the more he shrieked, the longer and the more hairy grew his ears.

A round, little Dormouse that lived upstairs was concerned to hear Pinocchio's screams and went to his room. Seeing Pinocchio so grief-stricken, she asked him anxiously, "What is the matter, dear little neighbor?"

"I am sick, my little Dormouse, very, very sick, from a disease that frightens me! Do you know how to take a pulse?"

"A little."

"Feel mine then and tell me if I have a fever."

The Dormouse took Pinocchio's wrist between her paws and felt his pulse for a minute. Then the Dormouse looked up at him sorrowfully and said, "My friend, I am sorry, but I must give you some very sad news."

"What is it?"

"You have a very bad fever."

"But what fever is it?"

"It's jackass fever."

"I don't know anything about that type of fever," said the puppet, realizing quite well, what was happening to him.

"Then I will explain it to you," said the Dormouse. "Within the next two or three hours, you will not be a puppet or a boy any longer."

"What will I be?"

"Within two or three hours you will become a real donkey, just like the ones that pull the fruit carts to market."

"Oh, what have I done? What have I done?" cried Pinocchio, grasping his two long ears in his hands and pulling and tugging at them angrily, just as if they belonged to another.

"My dear boy," answered the Dormouse to cheer him up a bit, "why worry now? What is done cannot be undone. Fate has deemed that all lazy boys who come to hate books and schools and teachers and spend all their days with toys and games must sooner or later turn into jackasses."

"But is it really so?" asked the puppet, crying miserably.

"I am sorry to say it is. Your tears are useless now. You should have thought of all this before."

"But the fault is not mine. Believe me, little Dormouse, the fault is all Lampwick's."

"And who is this Lampwick?"

"A classmate of mine. I wanted to return home. I wanted to be obedient. I wanted to study and to succeed in school, but Lampwick said to me, 'Why do you want to waste your time studying? Why do you want to go to school? Come with me to Play Land. There we'll never study again. There we can enjoy ourselves and be happy from morning until night.'"

"And why did you follow the advice of that untrustworthy friend?"

"Why? Because, my dear little Dormouse, I am a careless puppet . . . careless and heartless. Oh! If I had only had a bit of heart, I would never have abandoned my good Fairy, who loved me so well and who has been so kind to me! To think, by this time, I would no longer be a puppet. I would have become a real boy, like all my friends. Oh, if I meet Lampwick I am going to tell him what I think of him, and more, too!"

After this outburst, Pinocchio started to leave the room. When he got to the door, he remembered his donkey ears and turned back, feeling ashamed to show them in public. He took a long cotton cap and pulled it over his head, right to the tip of his nose.

He went out and looked for Lampwick everywhere. He searched for him along the streets, in the squares, in the theatres and every place, but he was not to be found. He asked everyone whom he met about him, but no one had seen him around. Finally Pinocchio went to his home and knocked at the door.

"Who is it?" asked Lampwick, from within.

"It is me!" answered the puppet.

"Wait a minute."

After a half an hour the door opened. Another shock awaited Pinocchio! There in

120

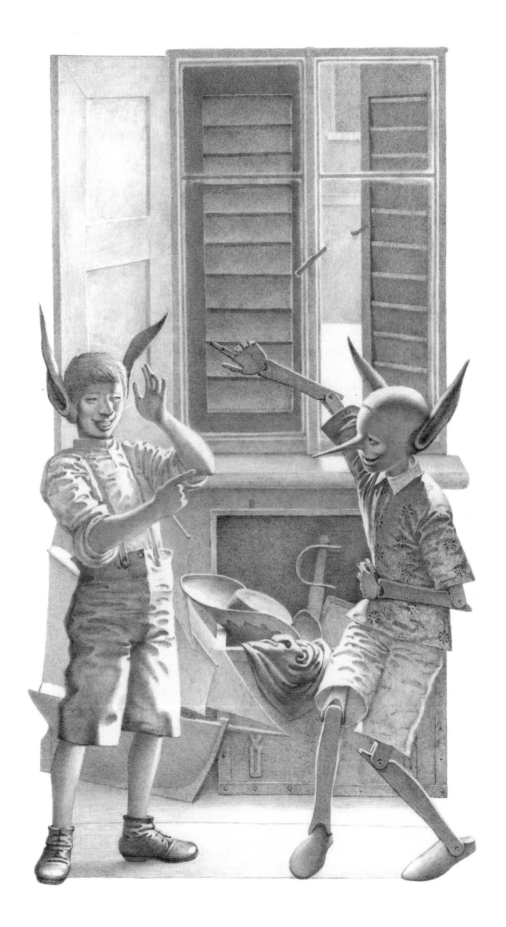

the room stood his friend, with a long cotton cap on his head, pulled down to the tip of his nose. The sight of that cap made Pinocchio feel slightly relieved. He thought, "My friend must be suffering from the same disease that I am! I wonder if he has jackass fever, too?" He pretended nothing was unusual, and inquired with a smile, "How are you, my dear Lampwick?"

"Very well! Like a mouse in a Parmesan cheese."

"Do you mean it?"

"Why should I lie to you?"

"Pardon me, my friend, but why then are you wearing that cap over your head?"

"The doctor prescribed it because I have scraped my knee. And you, dear puppet, why are you wearing that cap over your head?"

"The doctor prescribed it because I stubbed my toe."

"Oh, my poor Pinocchio!"

"Oh, my poor Lampwick!"

There followed an embarrassingly long silence, while the two friends stared at each other ridiculously. Finally, the puppet, in a voice sweet as honey and soft as a flute, said to his companion, "Tell me, Lampwick, dear friend, have you ever had anything wrong with your ears?"

"Never! And you?"

"Never! Still, ever since this morning, I have had an excruciating pain in my ear."

"I have the same complaint."

"You, too? And which ear is it?"

"Both of them. And yours?"

"Both of them, too. I wonder if it could be the same sickness."

"I'm afraid so."

"Will you do me a favor, Lampwick?"

"Gladly! With my whole heart."

"Will you let me see your ears?"

"Why not? But before I show you mine, I want to see yours, dear Pinocchio."

"No. You must show yours first."

"No, my dear! Yours first, then mine."

"Well, then," said the puppet, "let us make a compromise."

"Let's hear your compromise!"

"Let us take off our caps at the same time. Agreed?"

"Agreed!"

"Ready then?"

Pinocchio began to count, "One! Two! Three!"

At the word "Three!" the two boys pulled off their caps and threw them in the air.

Then something took place that would be hard to believe if it was not altogether true. When the puppet and his friend, Lampwick, saw that both of them were stricken by the same calamity, they did not feel sorrow and shame. Instead, they began to poke fun at each other, and after acting like a pair of buffoons, they ended by bursting into hilarious peals of laughter. They laughed and laughed and laughed until their sides ached.

Suddenly Lampwick stopped laughing. The color drained from his cheeks, and he struggled to keep his balance upright. Pale with fear, he turned and cried, "Help, help me, Pinocchio!"

"What is the matter?"

"Oh, help me! I cannot stand up straight."

"I can't either," cried Pinocchio, whose laughter turned to tears as he staggered about helplessly.

They had hardly finished speaking when both of them stumbled down on all fours and began running around the room. As they ran, their arms turned into legs, their feet turned into hooves, their faces lengthened into muzzles, and their backs took on a coating of gray fur. They wanted to cry and moan, overcome with grief and shame, but all they could do was bray loudly, "Hee-haw! Hee-haw! Hee-haw!" The poor creatures, so far reduced to the lowliest condition, were unbearably humiliated when tails began to grow out of their behinds.

At that moment, there was a loud knocking at the door and a voice called to them, "Open! It is Little Man, the driver of the wagon that brought you here. Open this door at once, or beware!"

CHAPTER XXXIII

Pinocchio becomes a donkey and is bought by the owner of a circus, who wants to teach him to do tricks. The donkey becomes lame and is sold to a man who wants to use his skin for a drumhead

Very sad and downcast were Pinocchio and Lampwick as they stood and looked at each other. Outside the room, the little man grew even more impatient, and finally gave the door such a violent kick that it flew open. With a fawning smile on his lips, he looked at them and said, "Good work, boys! You have brayed well, so well that I recognized your voices immediately, and here I am." On hearing this, the two donkeys bowed their heads in shame, lowered their ears, and put their tails between their legs.

At first, the Little Man stroked and patted them and smoothed down their hairy coats. Then he took out a brush and groomed them until they shone like glass. Satisfied with the appearance of the two little animals, he put a halter on them and took them to a market place far away from Play Land in the hope of selling them at a good price.

In fact, he did not have to wait very long for an offer. A farmer bought Lampwick, whose donkey had died the day before. Pinocchio was sold to the ringmaster of a circus, who wanted to teach him to perform tricks along with his other trained animals.

Now do you understand what was the Little Man's profession? This horribly unpleasant man, with his ingratiating smile, went about the countryside looking for boys. Lazy boys, boys who hated books, boys who wanted to run away from home, boys who were tired of school—all these were his joy and fortune. He took them with him to Play Land and let them enjoy themselves to the fullest. When they became donkeys, after months of all play and no work, he sold them on the market place. In a few years, he had become a millionaire.

What happened to Lampwick? My dear readers, I do not know. Pinocchio, I can tell you, met with great hardships from the first day.

After putting him in a stable, his new master filled his manger with straw, but Pinocchio, after tasting a mouthful, spat it out. Then the man filled the manger with hay, but Pinocchio did not like that any better. "Ah, you don't like hay either?" he cried angrily. "Wait, my pretty donkey, I'll teach you not to be so fussy." Without another word, he took a whip and gave the donkey a lash across the legs.

Pinocchio screamed with pain and as he screamed he brayed, "Hee-haw! Hee-haw! Hee-haw! I can't digest straw!"

"Then eat the hay!" answered his master, who understood the donkey's language.

"Hee-haw! Hee-haw! Hee-haw! Hay gives me a stomach ache!"

"Do you expect me to serve a donkey, like you, breast of chicken, or capon in aspic?" asked the man, growing angrier than ever and giving poor Pinocchio another lashing. After the second beating, Pinocchio shut his mouth and said no more.

The door of the stable was closed and Pinocchio was left alone. It was many hours since he had eaten anything and he started to yawn from hunger, with his mouth stretched open as wide as an oven. Finally, not finding anything else to eat in the manger, he nibbled a piece of hay. After a nibble, he chewed it well, closed his eyes, and swallowed it. "This hay is not bad," he thought. "But how much happier I would be if I had kept to my schoolwork! Just now, instead of hay, I would be eating a chunk of fresh bread and a tasty slice of salami. Patience!"

Next morning, when he awoke, Pinocchio looked in the manger for more hay, but it was all gone. He had eaten it during the night. He tried the straw, but, as he chewed away at it, he was disappointed that it didn't taste either like rice *alla milanese* or pasta *alla napoletana*. "Patience!" he reminded himself as he chewed. "If only my misfortune might serve as a lesson to disobedient boys who refuse to study! Patience! Have patience!"

"Patience indeed!" bellowed his master just then, as he came into the stable. "Do you think, perhaps, my little donkey, I have brought you here only to give you food and drink? Oh, no! You must help me earn some money. Do you hear? Come along, now. I am going to teach you to jump through hoops and to dance a waltz and a polka, and even to prance on your hind legs."

Poor Pinocchio, whether he liked it or not, had to learn all these wonderful tricks, but it took him three long months of training and many lashings that nearly cost him to lose his hide before he was considered perfect.

The day came at last when Pinocchio's master was able to announce an extraordinary circus performance. The announcement, posted all around the town in large letters, was written:

SPECTACULAR GALA EVENT

tonight

DARING ACROBATICS AND AMAZING FEATS PERFORMED BY THE GREAT ARTISTS AND CELEBRATED HORSES OF THE COMPANY

plus

Introducing

the famous

DONKEY PINOCCHIO

called

THE STAR OF THE DANCE

Entertainment and Lights Galore

126

That night, as you can well imagine, the theater was filled to overflowing an hour before the show was scheduled to start. There was not an orchestra or a balcony seat to be had, not even for the price of their weight in gold. The theater was swarming with boys and girls of all ages and sizes, jumping in their seats and fidgeting in anticipation of seeing the famous donkey Pinocchio dance.

When the first part of the gala was over, the circus ringmaster, wearing a black tailcoat, white knee breeches, and patent leather boots, presented himself to the audience, made a deep bow, and announced pompously, "Honored guests, ladies and gentlemen! As your humble servant, passing through this great metropolis, I have the auspicious honor and prodigious pleasure of presenting to this impressive audience a famous donkey that has formerly been granted the honor of performing before the kings and queens of all the principal courts of Europe. In thanking you all for granting us your animated presence, I kindly beg of you to favor us with your indulgence."

His speech was greeted with much laughter and applause. The applause grew to a roar when Pinocchio, the famous donkey, appeared in the circus ring. He was handsomely arrayed. A new bridle of shining leather with buckles of polished brass sat on his back, and two white camellias were tied to his ears. His mane was arranged in many curls, decorated with red silk ribbons and tassels. A great sash of gold and silver was fastened around his middle and his tail was decorated with ribbons of many brilliant colors. He was a donkey to win their hearts!

The ringmaster introduced Pinocchio, and added, "To our esteemed members of the audience! I shall not consume your time this evening in telling you about the enormous difficulties I encountered while trying to tame this animal, since I discovered him in the wilds of Africa. Observe, I beg of you, the savage look in his eyes. All the means used by centuries of civilization in subduing wild beasts failed in this case. I finally had to resort to the gentle language of the whip in order to bring him to my will. Despite all my kindness, however, I never succeeded in gaining his affection. He is still today as savage as the day I discovered him. He still fears and hates me. However, I have discovered there is one great redeeming feature about him. Do you see this little bump on his forehead? This bump is what gives him his great talent of dancing with the nimbleness of a human being and the ability to jump through hoops with ease. Admire him and let yourselves be entertained! I will let you be the judges of my success as this animal's teacher. Finally, just before I leave you, I wish to inform you that another performance will take place tomorrow night. If, in case, the weather threatens to rain, the great spectacle will start at eleven o'clock in the morning."

The ringmaster bowed deeply, and then he turned to Pinocchio and said, "Ready, Pinocchio! Before starting your performance, salute your audience!" Pinocchio obediently bent his two knees to the ground and remained kneeling until the ringmaster, with the crack of the whip, cried sharply, "Walk!"

The donkey lifted himself onto his feet and walked around the ring. A few minutes passed and again the voice of the ringmaster called, "Trot!" and Pinocchio obediently shifted his pace. "Canter!" he said, and Pinocchio quickened his pace. "Gallop!" and Pinocchio ran as fast as he could. "Charge!" and Pinocchio began to charge at full speed. As he sped around the ring, the master raised his arm and fired a pistol shot in the air. When the shot sounded, the donkey fell to the ground as if he were wounded and pretended to be dying.

A thundering burst of applause greeted the donkey as he rose to his feet. As the crowd cheered, Pinocchio raised his head to look around. There, in front of him, he saw a beautiful woman sitting in one of the box seats. She wore a long gold chain around her neck. A large medallion hung from the chain and on it, a picture was painted of a puppet.

"That picture is of me! That beautiful lady is my Fairy!" thought Pinocchio, recognizing her. He felt so happy and tried his best to cry out, "Oh, my Fairy! My own Fairy!" Instead of words, a loud braying was heard in the theater, so plaintive and loud that all the spectators, but especially the children, burst out laughing. Then, in order to teach the donkey that it was very poor manners to bray in front of an audience, the ringmaster struck him on the nose with the handle of the whip.

The poor little donkey stuck out a long tongue and licked his nose for a long time in an effort to take away the pain. What was his despair when he looked toward the boxes and saw that the Fairy had disappeared! He felt as if he might die. His eyes filled with tears, and he began to cry. No one was aware of it, not even the ringmaster, who cracked his whip and called out, "Bravo, Pinocchio! Now show us how gracefully you can jump through the hoops."

Pinocchio tried to jump two or three times, but each time he came near the hoop, he stooped and passed through underneath it. The fourth time, a stern look from his master forced him to leap through the hoop, but his hind legs caught in the hoop and he fell to the ground in a heap. When he got up, he was lame and could hardly limp to the stable.

"Pinocchio! We want Pinocchio! We want the little donkey!" shouted the boys from the orchestra, feeling sorry about the accident.

Pinocchio was not seen again that evening.

The next morning the veterinary — that is, the animal doctor — declared he would be lame for the rest of his life.

"What do I want with a lame donkey?" said the ringmaster to the stable boy. "Take this worthless animal to the market and sell him."

When they reached the market, a buyer was found at once. "How much do you ask for that lame donkey?" he asked.

"Twenty dollars."

"I'll give you twenty pennies. Don't think I'm buying him to work for me. I only want his hide. It looks tough enough to use for a drumhead. I belong to a village band and I want to make myself a drum."

I leave it to you, my dear readers, to picture to yourself the great pleasure Pinocchio

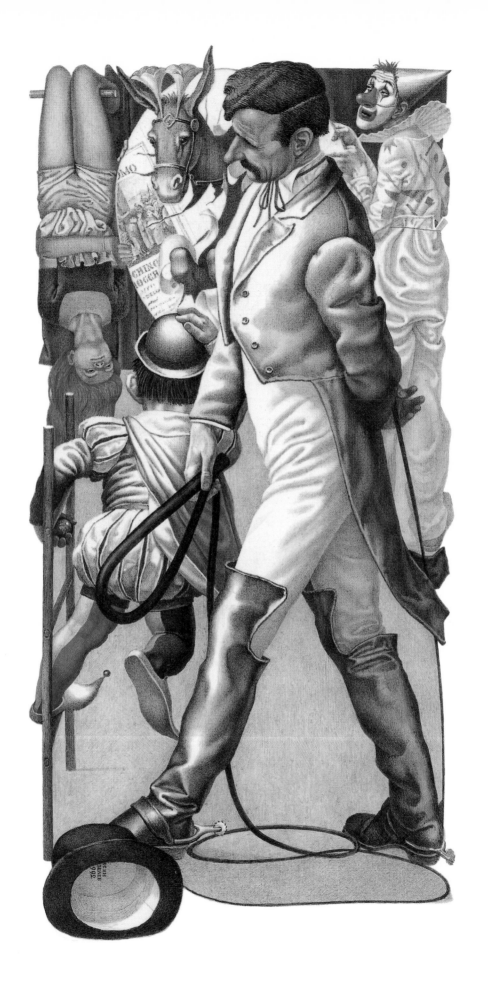

felt when heard that he was to become a drumhead!

As soon as the buyer had paid the twenty pennies, he led the donkey away to a cliff overlooking the sea. There he put a stone around the donkey's neck, tied a rope to one of his hind legs, gave him a shove, and threw him into the water.

Pinocchio quickly sank. His new master held onto the length of rope tightly, sat on the cliff, and waited for him to drown, so he could skin him and make himself a drumhead.

CHAPTER XXXIV

Pinocchio is thrown into the sea, eaten by fishes, and becomes a puppet once more. As he swims to land, the Terrible Shark swallows him

Down into the sea, deeper and deeper sank Pinocchio, and finally, after fifty minutes of waiting, the man on the cliff thought, "By this time my poor lame donkey must be drowned. Now I can drag him up and get to work on my beautiful drum." He pulled the rope which he had tied to Pinocchio's leg, and pulled and pulled and pulled until, at last, he saw appear on the surface of the water . . . Can you guess what? Instead of a dead donkey, he saw a live puppet that was wriggling and squirming like an eel.

Seeing that wooden puppet, the poor man thought he was dreaming and sat there like a dummy. He pulled his wits together and said, "What about the donkey I threw into the sea?"

"I am that donkey," answered the puppet laughing.

"You?"

"I."

"Ah, you little cheat! Is this a practical joke?"

"Practical joke? Not at all, dear master. This is a serious matter."

"But, then, how is it that you were a donkey a few minutes ago and now you are standing before me as a wooden puppet?"

"It may be the effect of salt water. The sea is fond of playing these tricks."

"Be careful, puppet, be careful! Don't scoff at me! I'm warning you, don't make me lose my patience!"

"Well, then, my master, do you want to know the whole story? Untie my leg and I can tell it to you better."

The old man, curious to know the true story of the puppet's life, released him immediately. Pinocchio, feeling free as a bird, began his story, "Once upon a time, I was a wooden puppet, just as I am today. One day I was going to become a boy, a real boy, but because of my laziness and my hatred of books, and because I listened to bad companions, I ran away from home. One beautiful morning, I woke up and discovered I had been changed into a donkey, with long ears, a gray coat, and a tail, too! What a shameful day for me! I hope you will never experience one like it, dear master.

"I was taken to the fair and sold to the ringmaster of a circus, who tried to make me dance and jump through the hoops. One night, during a performance, I had a bad fall and became lame. Not knowing what to do with a lame donkey, my master sent me to the market place and you became my new owner."

"Indeed I did! I paid twenty cents for you. Now who will return my money?"

"But why did you buy me? You bought me to do me harm . . . to kill me . . . to make a drumhead out of me!"

"Indeed I did! And now where will I find another donkey hide?"

"Never mind, dear master. There are a lot more donkeys in this world."

"Tell me, impudent rascal, is that the end of your story?"

"No," answered the puppet. "Two more words, and I am finished. After buying me, you brought me here to kill me. Feeling sorry for me, you preferred to tie a stone to my neck and throw me to the bottom of the sea. It was very humane of you to want me to suffer as little as possible and I will always be grateful to you, but now I expect my Fairy will take care of me . . ."

"Your Fairy? Who is she?"

"She is my mother and like all good mothers who love their children, she never loses sight of me, even though I am a brat and do not deserve it. Today my good Fairy saw me in danger of drowning, and sent a thousand fishes to me at the bottom of the sea. They thought I was really a dead donkey and began to eat me. What huge, greedy bites they took! One ate my ears, another my nose, a third my neck and my mane. Some went at my legs and some at my back, and among the others, there was one tiny fish so gentle and polite that he went so far as to eat my tail."

"From now on," said the man, horrified, "I swear I will never again eat fish. How I should enjoy opening a mullet or a whitefish just to find the tail of a donkey inside!"

"I agree with you," said the puppet, laughing. "I must still tell you that when the fish finished eating my donkey hide, which covered me from head to foot, naturally they came to the bones, or rather, to the wood in my case. As you can see, I am made of very hard wood. After the first few bites, those greedy fish realized that the wood was not good for their teeth and they were so sickened by such indigestible food, that they swam away without even saying goodbye. Now, dear master, you have my story. You know now why you found a puppet and not a dead donkey when you pulled me out of the water."

"I laugh at your story!" cried the man scornfully. "I know that I spent twenty cents for you and I want my money back. Do you know what I will do? I will take you back to the market and sell you as dry firewood."

"Very well, sell me. I don't mind," said Pinocchio, but as he spoke, he quickly dived into the sea. Swimming away as fast as he could, he cried out, laughing, "Goodbye,

master. If you ever need a skin for your drum, think of me." He swam on and on. After a while, he turned around again and called louder than before, "Goodbye, master. If you ever need a piece of good dry firewood, think of me."

In a few moments, he had gone so far that he could hardly be seen. All that could be seen of him was a very small black dot moving swiftly on the blue surface of the water, a little black dot that lifted a leg or an arm in the air now and then. One would have thought Pinocchio had turned into a porpoise playing in the sun.

After swimming for a long time, Pinocchio saw a large rock in the middle of the sea, a rock as white as marble. High on the rock stood a little goat bleating and calling to the puppet to come to her.

There was something very strange about the little goat. Her coat was not white or black or brown like any other goat, but blue, a deep brilliant color that reminded one of the Lovely Girl's hair.

Pinocchio's heart beat fast, and then faster and faster. He redoubled his efforts and swam as hard as he could toward the white rock. He was almost there, when suddenly a gruesome sea monster stuck its head out of the water, an enormous head with a huge jaw gaping wide open, with three rows of sharp, gleaming teeth, the sight of which would have made you shudder with fear.

Do you know what that sea monster was? It was none other than the Terrible Shark, often mentioned in this story. He was also nicknamed "The Attila of the Sea" by both fish and fisherman, because of his cruelty and the terror he spread.

Poor Pinocchio! The sight of that monster frightened him almost to death! He tried to swim away from him; to change his path, to escape, but its terrifying jaws kept coming nearer and nearer. "Faster, Pinocchio, please!" bleated the little goat on the high rock. Pinocchio swam desperately with all the strength in his arms, his chest, his legs, and his feet.

"Faster, Pinocchio, the monster is coming nearer!"

Pinocchio swam faster and faster, and harder and harder. "Faster, Pinocchio! The monster will get you! There he is! There he is! Quick, quick, or you are lost!"

Pinocchio went through the water like a shot, swimming faster and faster. He came close to the rock. The goat leaned over and held out one of her hoofs to help him up out of the water.

It was too late! The monster overtook Pinocchio and captured him. For a moment, the puppet was caught in rows of gleaming white teeth but then, the Shark took a deep breath and as he inhaled, he sucked in the puppet as easily as he would have sucked on a hen's egg. He swallowed him so hard that Pinocchio, falling down into the belly of the fish, lay stunned for a little while.

When he recovered his senses the puppet could not remember where he was. All around him was darkness, a dark so deep and so black that for a moment he thought he had put his head into an inkwell. He listened for a few moments and heard nothing. Now and again, a cold wind blew on his face. At first, he could not understand where the wind was coming from, but after a while he understood that it came from the monster's lungs. I forgot to tell you that the Shark was suffering from asthma and whenever he breathed, a storm seemed to blow.

Pinocchio at first tried to be brave, but when he became convinced that he was actually in the Shark's belly, he burst into sobs and tears. "Help! Help!" he cried. "Oh, poor me! Won't someone come to save me?"

"Who is there to help you, unhappy boy?" said a rough voice, like a guitar out of tune.

"Who is talking?" asked Pinocchio, frozen with terror.

"It is me, a poor Tuna swallowed by the Shark at the same time as you. And what kind of a fish are you?"

"I have nothing in common with fishes. I am a puppet."

"Then, if you are not a fish, why did you let this monster swallow you?"

"I didn't let him. He chased me and swallowed me without even saying 'please excuse me'! And now what are we to do here in the dark?"

"Wait until the Shark has digested us both, I suppose."

"But I don't want to be digested!" shouted Pinocchio, starting to cry again.

"Neither do I," said the Tuna, "but I am wise enough to think that if one is born a fish, it is better to die with dignity under the water than to die in shame in a frying pan."

"What nonsense!" exclaimed Pinocchio.

"It is my opinion," replied the Tuna, "and opinions should be respected."

"But I want to get out of this place. I want to escape."

"Go, if you can!"

"Is this Shark that has swallowed us very long?" asked the puppet.

"His body, not counting the tail, is almost a mile long."

While talking in the darkness, Pinocchio thought he saw a faint light in the distance.

"What can that be?" he said to the tuna.

"Some other poor fish, waiting as patiently as we are to be digested by the Shark."

"I want to see him. He may be an old fish and may know some way of escape."

"I wish you good luck, dear puppet."

"Goodbye, Tuna."

"Goodbye, puppet, and good luck."

"When will I see you again?"

"Who knows? It is better not even to think about it."

CHAPTER XXXV

In the Shark's belly, Pinocchio finds whom? Read this chapter and you will understand

Pinocchio had no sooner said goodbye to his good friend, the Tuna, than he began to walk away unsteadily in the darkness toward the faint light glowing in the distance. As he stepped along, he splashed his feet in puddles of such greasy and slippery water with the smell of fish fried in oil that Pinocchio thought it was the middle of Lent.

The farther he went the brighter and clearer grew the light flickering in the distance. He kept on and on until finally he reached it. What did he find? I give you a thousand guesses! He discovered a little table set for dinner and lit by a candle stuck in a glass bottle. Near the table sat a little old man, white as snow, eating some tiny, live fishes, so much alive that now and again one of them jumped out of the old man's mouth.

The sight of the little old man filled the puppet with a great delirium of happiness. He wanted to laugh, he wanted to cry, he wanted to say a thousand and one things, but all he could do was to stand still, stuttering and stammering brokenly. At last, with a great effort, he was able to let out a cry of joy and, opening his arms wide, he flung them around the old man's neck.

"Oh, father, dear father! Have I found you at last? Now I will never, never leave you again!"

"Are my eyes really telling me the truth?" answered the old man, rubbing his eyes. "Are you really my own dear Pinocchio?"

"Yes, yes, yes! It's me! Look at me! You have forgiven me, haven't you? Oh, my dear father, how good you are! Just think that I . . . oh my, if only you knew how many misfortunes have fallen on my head and how many troubles I have had! Just think that on the day you sold your old coat to buy me my ABC book so that I could go to school, I ran away to the Puppet Theater and the owner caught me and wanted to burn me to cook his roast lamb! He was the one who gave me the five gold coins for you, but I met the Fox and the Cat, who took me to the Inn of the Red Lobster. They ate like wolves

there, and I left the inn alone and met the murderers in the forest. I ran and they ran after me, always after me, until they hanged me to the branch of a giant oak tree.

"Then the Fairy of the Blue Hair sent the coach to rescue me and the doctors, after looking at me, said, 'If he is not dead, then he is surely alive,' and then I told a lie and my nose began to grow. It grew and it grew, until I couldn't get it through the door of the room. Then I went with the Fox and the Cat to the Field of Wonders to bury the gold coins. The Parrot laughed at me and, instead of two thousand gold coins, I found none. When the judge heard I had been robbed, he sent me to jail to make the thieves happy, and when I went away I saw that a nice bunch of grapes were hanging on a vine. The trap caught me and the farmer put a collar on me and made me a watchdog. He learned that I was innocent when I caught the weasels and he let me go.

The Serpent with the tail that smoked started to laugh and a vein in his chest broke and so I went back to the Fairy's house. She was dead, and the Pigeon, seeing me crying, said to me, 'I have seen your father building a boat to look for you in America,' I said to him, 'Oh, if I only had wings!' He said back to me, 'Do you want to go to your father?' and I said, 'Yes, but how?' and he said, 'Get on my back and I'll take you there.' We flew all night long, and next morning the fishermen were looking toward the sea, crying, 'There is a poor old man drowning,' and I knew it was you, because my heart told me so and I waved to you from the shore to come back . . ."

"I knew it was you, too," added Geppetto, "and I wanted to come back to you, but how could I? The sea was rough and the high waves overturned the boat. Then the Terrible Shark came out of the sea and, as soon as he saw me in the water, swam quickly toward me, put out his tongue, and swallowed me as easily as if I had been a little tortellini."

"And how long have you been trapped in here?"

"From that day to this, two long weary years—two years, my Pinocchio, which have been like two centuries."

"And how have you lived? Where did you find the candle? What about the matches to light it? Where did you get them?"

"You must understand that, in the storm which swamped my boat, a large ship also suffered the same fate. The sailors were all saved, but the ship went right to the bottom of the sea, and the same Terrible Shark that swallowed me, swallowed most of it."

"What! Swallowed a ship?" asked Pinocchio with surprise.

"In one gulp. The only thing he spat out was the mainmast, because it was stuck between his teeth. Fortunately, for me, the ship was loaded with meat, preserved foods, crackers, bread, bottles of wine, raisins, cheese, coffee, sugar, wax candles, and boxes of matches. With all that bounty, I have been able to survive well for two whole years, but now I am at the very last crumbs. Today there is nothing left in the cupboard, and this candle you see here is the last one I have."

"And then?"

"And then, my dear, we'll find ourselves in darkness."

"Then, my dear father," said Pinocchio, "there is no time to lose. We must try to escape."

"Escape! How?"

"We can run out of the Shark's mouth and dive into the sea."

"You mean well, but I cannot swim, my dear Pinocchio."

"Why should that matter? I'm a good swimmer. You can climb on my shoulders and I'll carry you safely to the shore."

"Dreams, my boy!" exclaimed Geppetto, shaking his head and smiling sadly. "Do you think it possible for a puppet, a yard high, to have the strength to carry me on his shoulders and swim?"

"Try it and see! In any case, if we are destined to die, then at least we will die together."

Without another word, Pinocchio took the candle in his hand and starting ahead to light the way, he said to his father, "Follow me and have no fear."

They walked a long distance through the belly and the rest of the Shark. When they reached the throat of the monster, they stopped for a while to wait for the right moment in which to make their escape.

I want you to know that the Shark was very old and, because he suffered from asthma and heart trouble, he was obliged to sleep with his mouth open. When Pinocchio looked out through the jaws of the sleeping Shark, he could see the night sky filled with stars.

"The time has come for us to escape," he whispered, turning to his father. "The Shark is fast asleep. The sea is calm and the night is as bright as day. Follow me closely, dear father, and we will soon be saved." With no time to spare, they climbed up the throat of the monster until they came to its immense open mouth. There they had to tread carefully because, if they tickled the Shark's long tongue, he might awaken and then what might happen? The tongue was so wide and so long that it looked like a country road. They were just ready to cast themselves into the sea, when the Shark sneezed suddenly and gave Pinocchio and Geppetto such a jolt that they were tossed backward and thrown once more into the belly of the monster. In their dilemma, the candle blew out and father and son were left in the dark.

"And now?" asked Pinocchio with a serious face.

"Now we are lost."

"Why lost? Give me your hand, dear father, and be careful not to slip!"

139

"Where will you take me?"

"We must try again. Come with me and don't be afraid."

Pinocchio took his father by the hand and, walking precariously, they climbed up the monster's throat for a second time. They crossed the whole tongue and jumped over three rows of teeth. Before they took the last great leap, the puppet said to his father, "Climb onto my shoulders and hold onto my neck tightly. I'll take care of everything else."

When Geppetto was securely holding onto his shoulders, Pinocchio, feeling very confident, made a dive into the water, and swam away from the Shark. In the moonlight, the sea appeared as smooth as oil and the Shark continued to sleep so soundly that even a cannon shot would not awaken him.

CHAPTER XXXVI

Pinocchio finally ceases to be a puppet and becomes a boy.

"My dear father, we are saved!" cried the puppet. "All we have to do now is to get to the shore." Without another word, he swam rapidly to reach land as soon as possible.

As Pinocchio lunged through the water, he noticed that Geppetto was shivering and shaking as if he had a high fever. Was he shivering from fear or from cold? Who knows? Perhaps it was a bit of both. But Pinocchio, thinking his father was frightened, tried to comfort him and said, "Courage, father! In a few moments we will be safe on land."

"Oh, but where is the blessed shore?" worried the little old man, squinting into the distance like a tailor threading a needle. "I am looking all around and can see nothing but sea and sky."

"I can see the shore," said the puppet. "Remember, father, I am like a cat. I see better at night than by day."

Poor Pinocchio pretended to be calm and reassuring, but he was far from feeling like that. He was beginning to feel discouraged, losing strength, and gasping for air. He felt he could not go on much longer, and the shore was still far away. A few strokes later, he turned to Geppetto and cried out weakly, "Save yourself, father! Help, for I am dying!"

Father and son were near to drowning when they heard a call from the sea, with a voice like an out of tune guitar "Who is dying?"

"My poor father and I."

"I know that voice. You are Pinocchio."

"Yes! And you?"

"I am the Tuna, your companion in the belly of the Shark."

"How did you escape?"

"I followed your example. You are the one who showed me the way. After your escape, I got away too."

"Tuna, you arrived just in time! Quickly, for the love of your tuna children, help us or we are lost!"

"With the greatest pleasure! Hang onto my tail, both of you, and let me lead. I'll have you both safe on land in no time at all."

Geppetto and Pinocchio, as you can easily imagine, did not refuse his proposal. In fact, instead of hanging onto the tail, they thought it better to climb on the Tuna's back.

"Are we too heavy?" asked Pinocchio.

"Heavy? Not at all, you are as light as sea-shells," answered the Tuna, which was as big and strong as an ox.

As soon as they reached the shore, Pinocchio was the first to jump to the ground to help his old father. Then he turned to the fish and said to him, "Dear friend, you have saved my father, and I have not enough words to thank you! Let me to embrace you as a token of my eternal gratitude."

The Tuna stuck his nose out of the water and Pinocchio knelt on the sand and kissed him fondly on his cheek. The poor Tuna was not accustomed to such outbursts of affection and was moved to tears. He felt so flustered that he turned about hastily and swam out to sea.

It was daybreak. Pinocchio offered his arm to Geppetto, who was so weak he could hardly stand, and said, "Lean on my arm, dear father, and let us go. We will walk very, very slowly, and when we feel tired we can stop and rest by the wayside."

"And where are we going?" asked Geppetto.

"To look for a house or a cottage, where someone will be kind enough to give us a piece of bread and some straw to rest upon."

They had not taken a hundred steps when they saw two grim creatures sitting by the road and begging for alms.

It was the Fox and the Cat, but in such a miserable state, they were hardly recognizable. The Cat, having pretended to be blind for so many years, had lost the sight of both eyes. The Fox, who had become thin and nearly bald, was without his tail. The sly old crook had fallen into the worst state of poverty and one day he had been forced to sell his beautiful tail for a morsel of food.

"Oh, Pinocchio," cried the Fox in a tearful voice. "Give us some alms, we beg of you! We are poor and invalid."

"Invalid!" repeated the Cat.

"So long, you rotten frauds!" answered the puppet. "You cheated me once, but you will never catch me again."

"Believe us! Today we are truly poor and starving."

"Starving!" repeated the Cat.

"If you are poor, you deserve it! Remember the proverbial saying, 'Stolen money never bears fruit.' So long, you rotten frauds."

"Have mercy on us!"

"On us!"

"So long, you rotten frauds. Remember the proverbial saying, 'Bad wheat always makes poor bread.'"

"Do not desert us."

"Desert us," repeated the Cat.

"So long, you rotten frauds. Remember the proverbial saying, 'Whoever steals his neighbor's coat, likely dies without a shirt.'"

Without further trouble, Pinocchio and Geppetto calmly went on their way. After a few more steps, they saw a pretty cottage made of straw, with a tile roof at the end of a lane. "Someone must live in that little cottage," said Pinocchio. "Let us see for ourselves." They went and knocked at the door.

"Who is it?" said a little voice from within.

"A poor father and a poorer son, without food and shelter," answered the puppet.

"Turn the key and the door will open," said the same little voice.

Pinocchio turned the key and, sure enough, the door opened. They went inside and looked all around, but found no one anywhere. "Is anyone here?" called Pinocchio.

"Here I am, up here!"

Father and son looked up to the ceiling and sitting there on a beam was the Talking Cricket.

"Oh, my dear Cricket," said Pinocchio, saluting him politely.

"Oh, now you call me your dear Cricket, but do you remember when you threw a hammer at me to kill me?"

"You are right, dear Cricket. Throw a hammer at me now. I deserve it! But spare my poor old father."

"I am going to spare both the father and the son. I only wanted to remind you of when you turned your back on me a long time ago, in order to teach you that in this world we must be kind and courteous to others, if we want to find kindness and courtesy in our own time of need."

"You are right, little Cricket, you are more than right, and I will remember the lesson you have taught me. But will you tell how you became the owner of this pretty cottage?"

"This cottage was given to me yesterday by a little goat with blue hair."

"And where did the goat go?" asked Pinocchio.

"I don't know."

"And when will she come back?"

"She will never come back. Yesterday she went away bleating sadly, and it seemed to me she said, 'Poor Pinocchio, I will never see him again. By now, the Shark must have eaten him.'"

"Is that what she really said? Then it was she . . . it was . . . my dear little Fairy!"

Pinocchio cried for a long time, wiped his tears, and made a comfortable bed of straw for old Geppetto and helped him to lie down. Then he said to the Talking Cricket, "Tell me, little Cricket, where might I find a glass of milk for my poor father?"

"Three fields away from here lives a farmer named Giangio. He has some cows. Go there and he might give you some milk."

Pinocchio ran all the way to Giangio's farmhouse. The farmer said to him, "How much milk do you want?"

"I want a full glass," said Pinocchio.

"A full glass costs a penny. First give me the penny."

"I haven't got a penny," answered Pinocchio, sadly.

"Very bad, my puppet," answered the farmer. "If you haven't got a penny, I haven't any milk."

"Too bad," said Pinocchio as he turned to leave.

"Wait a moment," said Giangio. "Perhaps we can come to an arrangement. Do you know how to work a waterwheel?"

"I can try."

"Then go to that well you see over there and draw me up one hundred buckets of water. After you have you have finished, I will give you a glass of warm sweet milk."

"All right."

Giangio led the puppet to the waterwheel and showed him how to pump the water. Pinocchio got to work but long before he had pulled up the one hundred buckets, he was completely tired out and dripping with sweat. He had never worked so hard in his life.

"Until today," said Giangio, "my donkey has done this work for me, but now the poor animal is sick and dying."

"Will you take me to see him?" said Pinocchio.

"If you like!"

When Pinocchio went into the stable, he saw a little donkey lying on a bed of straw. He was worn out from hunger and hard work. Looking at him intently, Pinocchio thought, "I know that donkey! I feel as if I've seen him before." He bent down and asked, "Who are you?"

The donkey opened his weary eyes and answered, "I . . . am . . . Lamp . . . wick." Then he slowly closed his eyes and died.

"Oh, my poor Lampwick," whimpered Pinocchio, as he wiped his eyes with a bit of straw he picked up from the ground.

"How can you feel sorry for a little donkey that has cost you nothing?" asked Giangio. "What about me? I am the one who have paid good money for him."

"But, you see, he was my friend."

"Your friend?"

"A classmate of mine."

"What?" shouted Giangio, bursting out laughing. "What? You had jackasses for classmates? What kind of an education did you have?"

The puppet felt so hurt and ashamed by those questions that he could not reply but accepted the glass of milk, and returned to his father.

From that day on, for more than five months, Pinocchio got up faithfully every morning just as dawn was breaking and went to the farm to draw water. Every day he was given a glass of warm milk for his poor old father, who grew stronger and better. Yet, he was still not satisfied. To earn money in his spare time, he learned to make baskets of reeds and sold them to pay for their necessities. He also built, among other things, a wheelchair for his father, and took him outside on nice days to enjoy the fresh air.

In the evening the puppet studied by lamplight to read and write. With some of the money he had earned, he bought himself a secondhand book with a few pages missing and taught himself to read in a very short time. For writing, he used a long stick that he sharpened into a pen. He had no ink, so he filled an inkpot with the juice of blackberries or cherries.

Slowly his ingenuity, hard work, and diligence were rewarded. He succeeded, not only in his studies, but also in his work, and a day came when he had enough money to keep his old father comfortable and happy. He was also able to save the great sum of fifty pennies to buy himself a new suit.

One day he said to his father, "I am going to the market to buy myself a coat, a cap, and a pair of shoes. When I come back I'll be so well dressed you will think I am a rich man." He ran out of the house and up the road to the village, laughing and singing. Suddenly he heard his name called, and looking around to see whose voice it was, and noticed a large Snail crawling out of a hedge.

"Do you recognize me?" asked the Snail.

"Yes and no. I'm not sure if I do."

"Do you remember the Snail that lived with the Fairy with Blue Hair? Do you not remember how she opened the door for you one night and gave you something to eat?"

"I remember it all," cried Pinocchio. "Answer me quickly, pretty Snail. Where have you left my Fairy? What is she doing? Has she forgiven me? Does she remember me? Does she still love me? Is she very far away from here? May I see her?"

After all these questions tumbled out one after another, the Snail answered as calmly as ever, "My dear Pinocchio, the Fairy is very sick in the hospital."

"In the hospital?"

"Yes, indeed. She has been stricken with trouble and poor health, and she hasn't a penny left to buy a piece of bread."

"Oh, how sorry I am! My poor, dear little Fairy! If I had a million, I would run to her with it! I only have fifty pennies. Here they are. I was just on my way to buy some clothes. Here, take them, little Snail, and give them to my good Fairy."

"What about the new clothes?"

"What does that matter? I would like to sell the rags I am wearing if it would help her more. Go, and hurry. Come back here within a couple of days and I hope to have more money for you! Until today, I have worked for my father. Now I must work for my mother also. Goodbye, Snail. I expect to see you again soon."

The Snail, contrary to her usual habit, ran away like a lizard under a summer sun.

When Pinocchio returned home, his father asked him, "Where is your new suit?"

"I didn't find one to fit me. I will look again some other day."

Pinocchio went to bed that night at midnight instead of ten o'clock and, instead of making eight baskets, he made sixteen. After that he went to bed and fell asleep. While he slept, he dreamed of his Fairy. She was beautiful, and kissed him, then smiled and said, "Bravo, Pinocchio! To reward you for your kind heart, I forgive all your mischievous ways in the past. Although they may not be models of obedience and good behavior, boys who always love and cherish their parents deserve to be praised and loved in return. Use your good sense, and be good in future, and you'll be happy."

At that very moment, Pinocchio awoke and opened his eyes wide. Just imagine his astonishment and happiness when he discovered that he was no longer a wooden puppet but had become a real, live boy! He looked all around and instead of the walls of straw, he saw the most remarkable room he had ever seen. He instantly jumped out of bed and found, next to it, a perfect new suit, a new hat, and a new pair of shoes all ready for him.

As soon as he was dressed, he put his hands in his pockets and pulled out a little leather purse on which were written these words: "The Fairy with Blue Hair returns fifty pennies to her dear Pinocchio with many thanks for his good heart." He opened the wallet and found, instead of fifty pennies, there were fifty gold coins!

Pinocchio ran to the mirror. He hardly recognized himself. A tall, dark-haired boy with a lively face smiled at him, with alert blue eyes, and he felt happy. In his bewilderment, he rubbed his eyes two or three times, wondering if he was sleeping or not, and decided he must be awake. "And where is my father?" he cried suddenly.

He ran into the next room, and there stood Geppetto, looking like his old self again, the wood carver Maestro Geppetto, hard at work as he embellished a finely made picture frame with leaves, flowers, and the little heads of animals.

"Father, father, what has happened? Tell me, please!" cried Pinocchio, who ran to his father and embraced him tightly and kissed him with great affection.

"You're the cause of all these sudden changes, my dear Pinocchio," answered Geppetto.

"What have I to do with it?"

"It's just this; when boys change from bad to good, they have the power to bring joy and happiness to their families."

"I wonder where the old wooden Pinocchio is hiding?"

"There he is," answered Geppetto. He pointed to a large puppet with a head turned to one side, arms dangling, and legs buckled, propped against a chair.

After looking at it for a very long time, Pinocchio thought, with a feeling of great fulfillment, "How ridiculous I was as a puppet! And how happy I am, now that I have become a real boy!"

The End

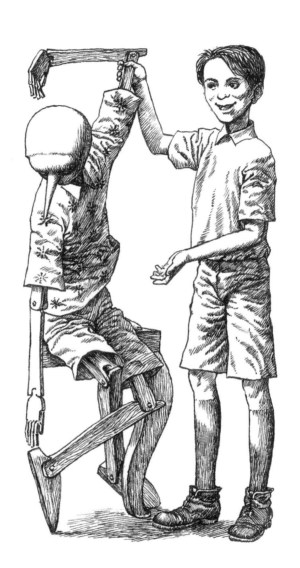

Printed and bound in Italy by Grafiche AZ, Verona
Printed on acid-free paper
Designed by Steedman Design, Vancouver

Pinocchio's body copy is typeset in Minion, designed by
Robert Slimbach. Minion is a fully developed neo-humanist
text face with unobtrusive texture but substantial x-height.
Minion's companion face, Poetica, also designed by Slimbach,
is used for the titles – Poetica Small Caps for the main titles,
and Poetica Chancery Italic for subtitles.

Carlo Collodi

Carlo Collodi was the pen name of Carlo Lorenzini, born in 1826 in Florence, the son of a cook and a servant, and the eldest of a large family. From his poor beginnings, Collodi was fortunate to receive an excellent education, with the financial support of benefactors who recognized his intellectual promise.

His career began in journalism, during the period of Italy's struggle to become an independent and unified state. A patriotic interest led him to establish two satirical-political newspapers and to enlist as a volunteer soldier. Although his principal occupation was in the civil service, his writing career continued, and covered a range of articles and essays on political and cultural subjects, and a few novels and plays.

Collodi's first work published for children arose from an opportunity to translate a collection of French fairy tales. He cultivated its success by making a departure from journalism in order to write books designed for use in schools and include his *Giannettino* series. In the newly established Italian state, Collodi became an innovator in the field of educational reform.

Following the popular success of his educational fiction and his retirement from the civil service in 1881, Collodi devoted his career to writing full-time for children. The story of Pinocchio first appeared as a serial in a children's newspaper, *Giornale dei bambini*. The complete story was published in 1883 to immediate success. The Adventures of Pinocchio is considered a masterpiece in Italian literature and remains a worldwide favorite among children.

Collodi died in 1890 and is buried in the town of San Miniato al Monte in Tuscany.

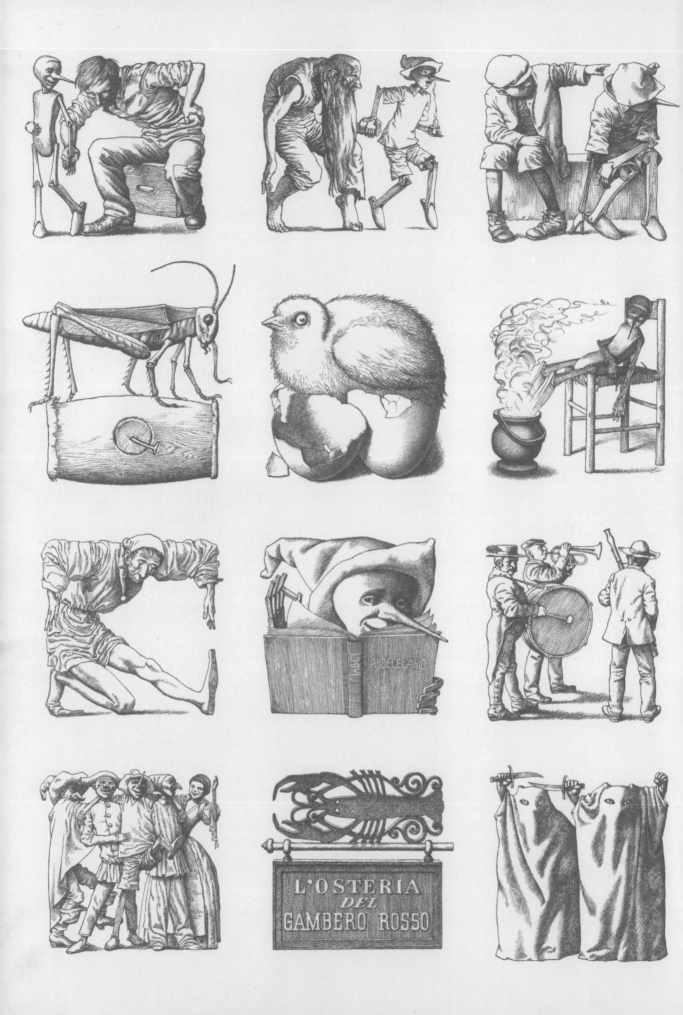